DARKMOOR

The Curse of Crow

To

Grace,

Enjoy,

Best wishes,

Matador
9 Priory Business Park,
Wistow Road
Kibworth Beauchamp
Leicester LE8 0RX, UK
Tel: (+44) 116 279 2299
Fax: (+44) 116 279 2277
Email: books@troubador.co.uk
Web: www.troubador.co.uk/matador

ISBN 978 1780885 568

British Library Cataloguing in Publication Data.
A catalogue record for this book is available from the British Library.

Typeset by Troubador Publishing Ltd, Leicester, UK

Matador is an imprint of Troubador Publishing Ltd

Printed and bound in the UK by TJ International, Padstow, Cornwall

Firstly, thank you to all the schools for your support, encouragement and enthusiasm towards the Darkmoor series.

Secondly, to my wonderful husband, and as ever my children: Nathan, Connor, Eve and Isobel. Thank you for keeping me going.

And thirdly, for anyone who has been awaiting Clever Crow's return…here *he* is!

Enjoy, Victoria x

www.darkmoorchildrensbook.co.uk

- PROLOGUE -

"I can just about make him out," Nathan whispered whilst narrowing his eyes to focus on the hairy beast.

"Is he on his own?" Jasmine asked as she placed an arrow on her bow.

"Yeah."

Anxiously, the six of them waited, holding their breaths as their hearts pounded with fear. All six of them knew that if they wanted to eat tonight, they would have to kill the beast.

It had been over a year since Matthew, Catherine and Sam had disappeared across the River of Souls, and with no sign of them returning Nathan had taken it upon himself to become the new leader of Camp Forgotten.

"He's getting closer, everyone hold your aim," Nathan instructed assertively.

The hairy wolf-lizard lifted his killer jaw-like-snout up into the gloomy air and inhaled. Then like lightning, out shot his deadly fiery tongue which thundered down onto the forest floor. The wolf-lizard sniffed up into the air as he smelt their sweaty human bodies, and then he let out a great howl.

Exhaling sharply, the wolf-lizard darted his black bulging eyes back and forth, then sniffing more rapidly, he roared out another bout of howls, for he knew exactly where those *meaningless* campers where hiding.

"Nathan," Claire whispered. "I think he's seen us."

"Wait-" Nathan muttered putting his arm across the front of Claire. "Just a little closer… ready… now!"

Immediately upon hearing his instruction, out of the dense woodlands jumped the six campers. Nathan, Claire, Jasmine, Andrew, Claude and Reuben, all with their arrows aimed at the beast ready to fire.

The wolf-lizard flashed out his tongue and began to whip it around his body in self defence. But he was out numbered six to one, and even with his flaming tongue and standing over eight feet tall, this wolf-lizard stood no chance against these six soldiers.

Not one, not two, but three arrows struck the beast, and instantly his rotten, hairy, smelly body crashed down onto the muddy floor. His eyes stared soullessly into space and his lizard tongue lay lifeless next to him. Not for the first time wolf-lizard was for dinner.

"Quick, let's get back to camp," Reuben called stepping over the beast's body and forcefully pulling out the arrows from his chest. Tossing them to one side, Reuben called again, "Come on, quick!"

The six of them each grabbed hold of the limp beast and heaved him up from the ground.

Silently, with their heads bowed, the six campers scurried back through the woods. Sweat trickled down their faces, not because of the heavy load but because they knew without a doubt, high up above, *he* would be watching.

And indeed *he* was. For every day since Matthew had left, *he* had watched the campers from high above the camp. His black coat had started to mirror the gloomy grey sky. His wings were beginning to look frail and tired as he spread them wide. But his deep, soulless, steely eyes stared down as cold as ever and that ear piercing caw was enough to make the six soldiers shiver.

"Don't look at him," Reuben muttered. "Let's just get back to camp."

"Yeah, come on," Claire encouragingly whispered.

The weight of the corpse was starting to slow them down, but determined to eat tonight they marched on. Up ahead the burning welcoming flames of camp blazed out from the two wooden pillars. As the huge wooden gates came more into view, high above the walls shot two flaming arrows.

"Hey, look, we're almost there!" Nathan shouted.

Crow hovered above, peering down at the commotion. He could see them, trying to hide their faces, not brave enough to look up at him. And even from this height, he could *smell* their fear. But they didn't really know him, they hadn't *yet* seen the real him, and as they quickly scampered back into the camp, Crow cawed.

He hovered for a few more moments. Then wrapping his wings tightly around his body and pointing his razor sharp beak up into the sky, Clever Crow shot off as fast as an arrow. Within seconds, Crow cut cleanly through the clouds and he spiralled heavenwards like a rocket.

Camp was now out of sight and so too was the land of Darkmoor. The air began to grow thin and no longer could the wind be felt against his tattered feathers. Crow effortlessly climbed higher and higher. Then there, in the blackness of the sky, a tiny star appeared to twinkle. Crow pushed on towards the light until it eventually became a huge ball. Once Crow was in touching distance, the starlight vanished, leaving an empty hole-like-window in the sky. Crow hovered for a moment, gazing through the window and into the world beyond. And there it was, positioned perfectly in view, like a framed picture, coated in a layer of snow, stood Crow's precious Victorian vicarage.

A sense of excitement rushed through him, and joyfully he flapped his wings. Clever Crow broke through the window, and immediately upon his exit the empty hole in the sky patched itself together, hiding away Crow's dark, deadly world.

He quickly glanced back, checking there was no trace of his masterful secret. Then soaring high above the winter wonderland of Filius, he felt the warmth of the winter's morning sunlight against his battered body, and instantly his black features were refreshed causing them to once again shine like silk. With his wings tucked in, Clever Crow began to freefall down through the icy air and down towards the Old Victorian vicarage.

- Chapter One -

Moving On

Matthew awoke to the sound of his dad's metal shovel grating along the rubble filled driveway. For the third morning in a row, Matthew's dad had been up early trying to clear the snow, only to re-awaken to another fresh coating. Undeterred however, Jack once again pushed the snow to one side in a bid to clear his driveway.

Meanwhile, Matthew lay warm under his bed covers, waiting for the alarm to ring. He didn't want to get up, not today, for today was *Thursday* and that meant only one thing; a full day at school followed by his weekly assessment with Doctor Wicks.

Today however, was Matthew's final assessment, for Doctor Wicks had promisingly said, "You're making excellent progress young man, and I think if this continues next week will be our *last* meeting!"

No one had believed him you see, not even his dad. After months of trying to convince everyone that Darkmoor *existed*, Matthew had been labelled the village nutter. Following months of name calling, his dad, Jack, was eventually forced into making Matthew see a *special* doctor.

After several appointments, Matthew had decided to pretend he'd made the whole thing up. He didn't like being picked on or ignored at school, so he put the memories of Darkmoor into the back of his mind and tried to move on. Matthew knew it would be difficult for people to believe in a world which was mastered by a transforming crow! Where mighty monsters lived! Where missing children hid in mud huts!

Even to Matthew it sounded fairy-tale-like. However, as much as Matthew tried to pretend his experiences never happened, the fact was, Darkmoor is *very* real. He knew that one day, Clever Crow would haunt him again and his nightmare would start over. But for now, Matthew was trying to get some normality back into his life.

He pulled his duvet away and stretched. Thankfully one of the earliest jobs he and Jack had done in the vicarage was to install a new central heating system. And since the snow had arrived, the boiler had been working overtime.

Matthew stood up and drew back his curtains. There, all wrapped up, was his dad shovelling the snow. Icicles had formed on the outside of his window and upon the wintery tree branches. Shivering at the frosty sight, he started to get ready for the school day ahead.

By the time Matthew had finished getting ready, Jack had finished his shovelling and was in the kitchen making breakfast.

"Good morning Matthew, you managed to get up then?" Jack asked teasingly.

"Yep!" Matthew smirked. "Have you managed to clear the driveway? I don't know why you bother Dad! The weather guy said to expect another load tonight."

"Son," Jack started as he cracked a couple of eggs into the frying pan. "I need to get the car out and besides its good exercise. And even better… the reward of a full *English* breakfast." Jack turned and patted his little tubby belly.

"Dad," Matthew chuckled, "what are you like?"

"Full English for you, Son?"

"No thanks, I'm not that hungry, I'll just have some bacon and eggs."

"Ok Son, kettle's just boiled," Jack said, prompting Matthew to make use of himself. Jack returned back to the frying pan and turned over the rashers of bacon before adding in a couple of eggs.

Matthew took two cups out of the cupboard and dropped a teabag in each, spooned in a couple of *heaped* sugars and poured in some freshly boiled water.

3

"Hmm… Matt, you haven't forgotten about your appointment later today, have you?" Jack asked whilst flipping over the bacon once more.

"Nope," Matthew answered back.

"Good, good, cause you know what the doctor said about you making progress – "

"Yes Dad, I know. Then at last, well, hopefully I'll be officially classed as *normal.*"

Jack turned to face his son, "Matthew!"

"What?" Matthew said shrugging his shoulders. "That's what you want, isn't it? A *normal* son?"

"Son, don't start this now, we have gone over this a hundred times – "

"Yeah, and you still think I'm mad, just like the rest of the villagers. You think I'm as crazy as Mum."

"Son," Jack spoke calmly. "I don't think *you're* mad, just… you know, you have an over-active imagination. Come on Matt, even Doctor Wicks said that. And besides your mum, well, she wasn't *crazy* either, she just… " his voice trailed off as he remembered Matthew's mum. Looking down at the floor, Jack sighed before continuing, "She just couldn't cope with you… and I guess she just fell out of love with me and one day, well you know," Jack swallowed hard before continuing, "she just left."

Matthew could see the sadness in his dad's eyes. He'd seen it there many times before, and Matthew could almost hear his dad's heart breaking all over again.

Turning to stir the cups of tea, Matthew softly spoke, "I'm sorry Dad. I know it must've been really hard for you when she left. It's just… I thought she was a good person?"

"She was Matthew –"

"Then why? Why would she just leave us, Dad? Is there something you're not telling me?"

"Like what?" Jack turned towards Matthew, with a confused, crumpled frown expression on his face. "What would I *not* be telling you? Just accept it Matthew, your mum left because she wasn't happy, obviously she no longer loved me, that's it."

Jack moved towards Matthew and placed his hand upon his son's sunken shoulders. "Matthew," he spoke in a whisper. "Look at me Matty. Why would I lie to you? I know it's hard to understand, but I swear to you –"

Matthew, still unconvinced, looked up into his dad's eyes and whispered, "Please Dad, just tell me the truth."

"I am Matthew. I don't fully understand why she left us, I mean falling out of love with me, maybe one day I'll understand. But you… Matthew, you have to let this go, she's gone and she's not coming back, ok?"

Matthew just nodded. He so desperately wanted to understand why his mum would just leave, but he would never understand it. Now, *eleven* years on, the pain was not getting easier, instead the more he seemed to grow up, the more questions he wanted answering.

"I just wanted to understand Dad. I guess –"

"I know Son, and I swear if I knew anything else I would tell you, you have to believe me. You didn't even know her –"

Matthew quickly looked at Jack, stuttering over his words, he asked, "What… what did you say?"

"I said you didn't even know her," Jack slowly repeated his last words. "What?"

Matthew's legs grew weak beneath him. Reaching out to grab the worktop, he shut his eyes tight.

Those words, those five words seemed so familiar. Over and over again he repeated the words in his head: *"You didn't even know her."*

Where? Where had he heard them before? Not from his dad, no, from someone else, somewhere else. He tried hard to remember, he tried to picture who, where… but nothing.

Opening his eyes wide, Matthew looked at his dad, "I'm sorry, Dad. I'm sorry she left you to bring me up –"

"Don't *ever* apologise for that Matthew, you're the only thing I have and I love you very much, don't ever forget that."

"Now… " Jack said swallowing hard. "Let's have that breakfast."

Matthew nodded, and a tiny smirk appeared from the corner of his mouth. He placed both cups of tea down on to the breakfast bar and perched himself up on one of the stools. Jack placed a plate of bacon and eggs down in front of him, and then hopped onto the stool opposite his son, before tucking into his full English. Reaching across the bar, Jack started to unfolded his morning newspaper.

"Hey Matt," Jack spluttered, "I told you Crow would be back."

Matthew quickly looked up. The mention of *his* name made Matthew's heart race. His stomach performed somersaults as he sharply asked, "Who?"

"Crow," Jack repeated. Slowly looking over the top of his paper, Jack continued, "You know, Darren Crow? Footballer for Filius… "

"Matty, are you ok? You look like you've seen a ghost?" Jack asked concerned, as Matthew sat staring vacantly towards him.

Just about managing a smile, Matthew faintly answered, "Yeah, yeah I'm fine. Look I'm gonna walk to school today, I promised to meet Cassie anyway so… " Matthew said jumping up off his stool and grabbed his coat and bag.

With a mouth full of food, Jack asked after him, "What about your breakfast?"

"I'm not hungry, you have it!" Matthew called back as he walked down the hallway towards the front door.

Glancing over his shoulder, he saw Jack sliding his plate across the bar, and without looking up from his paper, he called, "Bye Son, see you tonight and don't forget –"

But Matthew had already gone. Hearing the front door slam shut, Jack muttered to himself, "Your appointment with the doctor."

Matthew stood on the doorstep watching the snowflakes swirling down onto the ground. Instantly the cold air closed in around him, his icy breath drifted up like white clouds into the snow filled sky above. Matthew stood there for a few more moments, then zipped up his coat and stepped off the step. Slowly he trudged across the front garden, leaving shoe imprints on the top of the crunchy snow. An overwhelming sense that he was being watched suddenly rushed over him. He turned to look back at the vicarage, wondering if his dad would be stood waving him off, but no one was there.

However, unbeknown to Matthew, from high upon the chimney stack, someone was indeed watching. He was just waiting for the right moment to reveal himself, waiting for the right moment to once again restart Matthew's living nightmare. Teasingly and with a great deal of intimidation, he let out a gentle but familiar caw.

Immediately Matthew dropped his bag and slowly turned his head to look back towards the vicarage.

"No!" Matthew shouted, as he stood motionless in the middle of the garden. Then standing still, his heart pumped uncontrollably. Feeling completely exposed to the world around him, he closed his eyes tight.

A picture quickly flashed within his mind, a face? No, that wasn't it. He stood bewildered, his eyes firmly shut. Once again the picture flashed before him. Trying hard to block out everything else around him, he focused on the blurred image inside his head. What was it? Who was it?

"Matthew, Matthew, you ok?" an angelic voice called, disturbing his thoughts.

The angel reached out to take hold of his hand.

"Matthew."

Cautiously he opened his eyes, and there standing in front of him was a girl.

"Catherine?" Matthew whispered trying to focus on her face.

"No Matthew, its Cassie!" Cassie replied flippantly, pulling away her warming touch from his.

"Cassie?" Matthew asked confused.

"Yes, you know… your *best* friend!" Cassie said. "What on earth are you doing?"

Matthew studied Cassie's face. Her pale skin was almost camouflaged against the snowy backdrop, her chocolate coloured eyes stared angrily back at him, and her dark brown hair was beautifully brushed down over her shoulders and fell down her back.

"Well!" she demanded, firmly crossing her arms across her chest, clearly still annoyed at for him calling her the *wrong* name.

Matthew couldn't help but grin at her miffed expression, "I thought I heard something, someone," Matthew stopped and looked back towards the vicarage. Shaking his head, a grin which spread the width of his face appeared.

"I guess I must be going mad!" he joked as he bent down to pick up his bag.

"Don't say that, you've just about proved to everyone you're not!" Cassie said trying her hardest not to smile back at him.

Placing her hand back into his, they started walking towards the road, "Come on, speed up!" Cassie called, forcefully pulling him along. "We don't want to be late for school."

"No, you're right," Matthew replied and together they walked quickly along Acerbus Road, heading off in the direction of Filius High.

Crow was still watching. A feeling of anger came

over him. Matthew was different somehow, and this *new* girl, she *liked* him?

Crow continued to watch as they walked hand in hand down Acerbus road, not *once* did Matthew look back at the vicarage.

Crow had been waiting for over a *year* to return to Filius. He'd hoped in his absence that Matthew would have been classed as crazy, the village outcast, just like he had been labelled for all of those years he'd lived in the vicarage. But *nothing* had prepared Crow for this. Matthew appeared as though he'd moved on, as if he'd forgotten about everything that had happened to him. He didn't seem mad *or* crazy, and he certainly wasn't an outcast, flaunting around with this *new* girl!

Unfortunately for Crow, he didn't know that Matthew *had* been labelled the village nutter. And unbeknown to everyone in Filius, Matthew was just pretending he'd forgotten about Darkmoor, just so he'd fit in. And unbeknown to Matthew, Crow had fallen for his act too.

As Crow watched him, he could feel anger raging up inside of him. In temper Crow opened up his wings and cawed aggressively down into the village below. Then hopping up off the chimney, he looped several times around the old Victorian vicarage before darting up into the heavens above.

He didn't stop once as he slammed through the winters sky and back into Darkmoor. Angrily he glared down at *his* world below. He instantly recognised the bellows of smoke which puffed out of camp into the black sky. For a moment he thought of causing havoc for the campers, but instead he dived down and flew along the muddy riverside, flying only an inch or so from the ground. As he rocketed over the white misty river, his majestic angels lifted themselves gracefully out of the mist and called excitedly towards their master. Crow danced on the airwaves between them, the white mist wrapping itself around their bodies. Like dolphins, Crow and his angel dived in and out of the River of Souls. Once he'd reached the other side, the angels began to cackle at one another, ruby red blood pouring from their mouths as they worshipped their master.

Carrying on up through the graveyard he flew. Occasionally glancing down at the graves he'd dug, then he whizzed through the rotten rusted gate. Eventually, there upon the hillside he could see his kingdom, his castle. The candlelight flickered calling him home, and as Crow touched down on the hillside, his warming, welcoming fog immediately wrapped itself around him.

Crow stretched out his wings wide, and unfolded his fingers from beneath them. Curling up his beak, his tiny beady eyes grew wide. From the back of his head, his feathers multiplied, over lapping each other, they lengthened down his back and onto the floor. His razor sharp claws cracked and fell off. The fog grew evermore dense around him. Faster and faster it swirled, like a tornado. No noise was made from either him or the fog, but silently, the amazing, magical transformation, in which Darkmoor had done a hundred times before, was complete. The fog, snake-like, slowly slithered away and there stood Darkmoor.

He plucked a few leftover feathers from the back of his overcoat, creaked his neck from side to side, and looked down at his newly formed fingers, ensuring all ten where there. He swept his dark sleek hair away from his long narrow face and revealed those deadly steely eyes.

Stern faced, Darkmoor stood proud. His lips were firmly pushed together, and his face was colourless as he lifted his head up towards the sky. He stood still for only a moment, before he marched off up the hillside, towards the castle. The ground thundered beneath him with every step he took. All the while his eyes widened in size and deepened in colour.

Darkmoor placed his foot on the top step and quickly turned around to look back down the hill. From here he could see the whole land which he had created. With a clap of his hands he could command the skies above him. From one simple word off his lips, a whole army of wolf-lizards could appear and obey everything he would command. From up here, on the top of this hill, in front of *his* castle, Darkmoor was both King and Master, and Matthew *would* come to obey him.

With that thought, without a moment's hesitation, Darkmoor marched purposefully towards the only person that could help him in his quest, *Catherine*.

- Chapter Two -

Catherine's Torment

"Catherine! Oh Catherine! Where *are* you?" Darkmoor called teasingly, as he walked along the cobbled pathway and through the narrow candle lit arch.

Suddenly he stopped, that evil grin grew wide across his face, "Oh *that's* right, you're in *my* dungeons."

He turned sharply to face the dark stairwell which disappeared down into the dungeon below. He removed a burning torch from its holder on the wall, stretched it out in front of him, and let the burning flames light up the way to Catherine's cell. Stepping onto the first step, he called down, "Catherine, I have some news for you!"

Catherine heard his voice. She'd gotten use to that raw gravel tone he used when he was feeling his *most* callous. She had become so weak and tired that she didn't try answering back anymore. All her fight and fierceness had long drained away. The skeleton like body of Catherine sat there on the hard cold floor. Her ankles were blistered and bruised from the chains which kept her captive in her cell. She wrapped her arms tightly around her frail body, trying to stop herself from shivering.

Then, from up above, she heard his heavy black boots. Every step taken was accompanied by a vicious flicker of candlelight, which illuminated the damp walls. She looked up towards the ever growing light, anticipating Darkmoor's appearance.

First his boots came into view, coated in a layer of dried mud. Then up from his boots his long black coat came into view, swaying rapidly from side to side. In the early days Catherine had teased him about his dress sense: only ever wearing, what she'd nicknamed, his *Black Rain Mac*, but she'd no energy now. She didn't ever try to engage in any sort of conversation with him.

Continuing to make his way down into the dungeon, he called her name over and over again. This was something he *always* did, and she could never work out why. Maybe it was his way of teasing her *or* reminding himself of who she was?

Catherine watched and waited.

Placing her head upon her knees, she could feel her heart pounding inside of her chest. Hearing his voice had become comforting and warming. There was part of her that sprung to life whenever he was near, and she knew for certain that every time he left the castle, he would return back to her, something *Matthew* hadn't done. In Catherine's mind, Matthew had abandoned her, left her for dead, but Darkmoor, he always came back.

The torchlight became brighter as his footsteps grew louder. Catherine looked up, and there he stood. Every feature on his face was aglow in the light. Every day he seemed to grow taller as he towered over her, and every day she'd hoped it would be her last in this dreary, depressing place. But deep down, she knew, with that cold icy stare in his eyes, her final day might never come.

She shuffled herself towards the back of the cell. Dust drifted up from the floor causing her to cough, and quickly she placed her hand over her mouth to block out any unwanted dirt. Pushing herself back against the steel bars, she shut her eyes and prayed for this misery to finally end.

Darkmoor began brushing his long bony fingers across the bars, followed by an evil eruption of laughter.

"Catherine, oh Catherine, don't hide back there. Don't you want to hear my news?"

He waited for a moment but Catherine didn't respond.

"Catherine!" he shouted aggressively. "Catherine, come here into the light!"

But still Catherine didn't respond.

"Catherine," Darkmoor called again. "If you don't come here, I can't tell you my news and I think you will *love* this."

Catherine slowly unfolded her arms and stretched them out. Her bones ground together as she placed her hands flat onto the floor, ready to push herself up. Her body was fragile, frail and weak, and her clothes which she'd worn every day for over a year, were smelly, old and torn. She had taken her shoes off one day and in temper she'd thrown them through the bars at Darkmoor. They'd missed, of course, and he had just left them there to decay. With a mighty effort she stood wearily, and slowly dragged her feet across the floor. The chain which was holding her captive, grated and clattered along behind her. She managed to lift her head up to face him determined not to show him her weakness and vulnerability. As she shuffled further forward, Catherine felt the warming, fiery glow of the torchlight upon her face. As she brushed her greasy red curls away from her eyes, clumps of it fell away in her hand, tossing her dead hair down onto the floor, she continued towards him.

"Oh my darling Catherine, you look happier every day," Darkmoor snarled.

Not wanting to give him eye contact, she let her eyes get lost in the dancing flames of the torch. Freely the flames danced, unaware of the cruel, dark, deadly man in which they were being held.

Darkmoor placed a hand through the bars and touched Catherine's cheek. Gently he stroked it, and slowly Catherine turned her head away.

"You said… " Catherine muttered, "… you've got some news?"

She still didn't look up at him, she wasn't frightened of him, not anymore. At first she was petrified of him, those black soulless eyes, that taunting voice of his and that icy touch of his upon her face. But now, now she felt nothing.

Darkmoor stepped back from the cell and stared at her. Then he whispered, "I've been to see Matthew."

Instantly, at the mention of his name, Catherine's heart beat fast, injecting some life into her weary body. Now, this time, she *did* look up at him.

"Matthew," she faintly gasped, before innocently asking, "has he come back for me?"

"Oh, Catherine that's so sweet, no he's not come back for you," Darkmoor mocked. "He's still in Filius."

Darkmoor turned away from her. With the torchlight in hand, he marched up and down the dungeon, swaying the torch from left to right as if deep in thought.

Catherine slumped down to the floor. The raw cut emotions she had felt over a year ago when Matthew had left her, resurfaced once more. She wrapped her arms back around her body, and sitting in the dark shadows, Catherine cried.

Darkmoor, unaware of Catherine's tears, muttered to himself. His voice grew angrier by the second as his footsteps pounded the floor. Then swiftly he turned back to Catherine's cell and shone the torch through the bars.

"Oh Catherine, there's no need to cry! Well, not yet anyway, I haven't told you the best bit. He appears to have forgotten all about us, well, I can understand him forgetting you but me! How dare he? And he's even got a *new* girlfriend!"

"What?" Catherine whispered wiping her tears away.

"Yes," Darkmoor replied in a matter of fact manner. "Dancing and joking around, so I think it's time he remembered exactly what happened," Darkmoor's eyes narrowed. Staring down at Catherine he asked, "Don't you?"

Catherine quickly darted her eyes across the dungeon floor, immediately knowing what Darkmoor wanted. She reached out her legs and stretched out her toes in an attempt to reach it but her efforts were hopeless.

"Now now Catherine, you know what will happen if you don't give me what I want… " Darkmoor said watching a defenceless Catherine puffing and panting, trying desperately to grasp her most precious possession.

"No!" Catherine shouted. "You can't have it!"

"Oh but my dear, I think you'll see… that I can!"

Left unloved, uncared for and buried underneath a thick pile of dust, was Catherine's diary. In a raging outburst, she had thrown it against the cell bars and it had landed face down on the cold floor, where it had remained… until now.

She had buried her feelings deep down inside of her. The love and affection she once had for the diary had over time turned into hate. But something started welling up inside of her, slowly bubbling away, was it the love she once had returning?

She tried even harder to reach it, as the thought of Darkmoor taking her diary away from her was unbearable, and although she knew she would probably never write in it again, she could feel a fiery temper rising up inside.

"No!" Catherine shouted again. "Please no!"

"Please no!" Darkmoor mockingly replied. "Catherine, I'm only borrowing it for a while, and then *I promise* you can have it back." And with that, he bent down low whilst staring Catherine in the eye, and carefully positioned his hand between the bars.

"There we go," Darkmoor spoke calmly. He dusted off the top layer of dirt and revealed Catherine's diary.

"Please," Catherine pleaded. "It's all I have."

Although she had tried to convince herself that somewhere deep inside of him was a heart, his actions towards her said otherwise, and for some reason, he was out for revenge.

He didn't speak to her again, as his dagger eyes darted from the diary to Catherine. He clamped his hand around the book and slowly dragged it across the floor.

Catherine's fragile body drained of all energy as she slumped down onto the dungeon floor. The torchlight quickly disappeared as Darkmoor purposefully made his way back up the stairwell, taking with him *all* of Catherine's secrets.

Upon reaching the top step, Darkmoor glanced back down the well. For a split second a rush of pity came over him, and then just for a moment those steely black eyes softened.

"I'm sorry Catherine," he whispered to himself, but with one blink of his eyes the softness vanished. Placing the diary under his arm, he headed off across the Roman theatre and towards his chamber.

Slamming the iron door shut, Darkmoor gripped the diary so tight that his fingers became numb. Still grasping the flaming torch in his other hand, he swiftly set about lighting the other torches until his dark dusty room lit up. Finding an empty torch holder, Darkmoor finally released his grip and slid the flaming torch into it.

"Now look what I've got," he proclaimed proudly, staring deep into a corner of the room.

Perfectly still, wrapping her wings tightly around her delicate body, not allowing one ounce of light to shine from her beautiful white coat, was Dove. Like ice she froze her gaze upon him, and the closer he stepped towards her, the tighter her stare became.

"Do *you* want to see?" he asked teasingly, holding up Catherine's diary in front of her. Dove remained motionless.

Dove's silver cage was once more holding her captive. However, Darkmoor had learnt his lesson and made sure she remained in his room, securely locked away from the outside world.

After rescuing Matthew from Darkmoor's castle, Dove feared she would finally feel the full force of Darkmoor's wrath.

"Shall we read it?" Darkmoor asked with a false sense of excitement aimed at further unsettling Dove.

A wicked smirk flashed across his face, he turned away from Dove and proceeded to walk across the room, before sitting down at his stone table.

He tossed the diary carelessly down. Dust spiralled up into the air and tickled the burning flames. After a thorough wipe, the pink aging cover was revealed. He carefully moved his fingers over the embossed words, which read: *Catherine's Diary*.

He paused for a moment. Hesitantly he began to turn the first cover then suddenly closed it. Did he really want to read about her past? Would he be in there? He coughed to clear his throat as the memories of him and Catherine at the Vicarage came flooding back. He pictured her face smiling towards him from her bedroom window.

Darkmoor quickly gathered his thoughts and forcefully flung open the book.

- Chapter Three -

Classroom Commotion

"Matthew Khan! Are you listening to me?" a woman's voice bellowed across the classroom, causing most of the children to sit bolt upright in their chairs.

Again Mrs Summers shouted, "Matthew Khan!"

Matthew appeared to be in some sort of a daydream, his eyes twitched every so often as he watched tiny snowflakes fall from the grey clouds above.

Running out of patience, Mrs Summers barked like a Sergeant Major, "Matthew Khan, for the third and final time, will you *stop* looking out of the window and pay attention!"

Nearly all of the pupils of Filius High secretly referred to Mrs Summers as: *The old battleaxe*. She was built like an ox. The muscles in her upper arms bulged out from under the sleeves of her white blouse, and her hands were the size of dinner plates. Her strawberry blond hair was always scraped back tightly into a bun, as though it was glued on the top of her head. Mrs Summers' deep gruffly voice could be heard throughout the whole school, occasionally causing some of the other teachers to shudder in disbelief at the level of noise that one human being could produce. Never once did she wear a pair of high heel shoes rather she wore brown knee high boots, the tops of which touched the hem of her blue pencil skirt.

"Psss, Matthew," Cassie whispered from behind, poking Matthew with her HB pencil, "Mrs Summers is calling you."

Feeling the sharp prod, Matthew quickly turned around to face Cassie.

"What are you doing?"

Without saying a word, Cassie raised her eyebrows and nodded towards the front of the class.

Mrs Summers stood with her arms tightly crossed across her manly chest. She was frantically hammering a heavy foot down onto the floor, causing some of the children's table legs to dance under her mighty force. Once more, *the old battleaxe* boomed across the class towards Matthew.

"Earth calling Mr Khan!"

Frowning at Cassie, Matthew slowly turned around in his chair. Not looking up at his teacher, he sheepishly apologised, "Sorry Miss."

"Hmm!" Mrs Summers muttered. "Well, let's get started, shall we?"

She picked up her whiteboard pen, flipped off the top and began to write the date across the board.

"Right class, today we are going to start our new topic, a critical analysis regarding the differences between fiction and non-fiction."

Cameron Thomas (who was sat in front of Matthew) sniggered under his breath, "Matthew will be good at this."

Cameron Thomas, aka: *The classroom bully,* had his own little tribe of groupies, made up of the younger, vulnerable children in the school. He relished in his reputation of being the *cockiest* boy at Filius High and would deliberately misbehave in class. He'd walk around the school corridors with his uniform intentionally scruffy, in the hope he could get his *behaviour* card full of crosses. He constantly refused to remove his diamond earring and his chunky silver chain. On one occasion, poor Mr Rigby, the PE teacher and the school's football team coach, was left with no choice but to send him directly to the head teacher's office. Somehow though, despite Cameron's troubles, Mr Rigby had often picked him for the football team, to the bewilderment of Matthew and the other boys in the squad.

Cameron had had it in for Matthew every since he'd moved to Filius, teasing him about his, so called, *magical adventure and talking bird!* And ever since Matthew and Cassie had become *good* friends, Cameron had done everything he could to wind Matthew up. So far, much too Cameron's annoyance, Matthew hadn't bitten. But today Matthew felt different, strange, as if at any moment, something, anything could happen.

Cameron threw a sly smirk at him, and slowly an overwhelming anger bubbled up within Matthew, and for a moment he held Cameron's stare. They stared at each other, both determined not to blink first.

Cameron pursed his lips, "What? Have I hit a nerve?"

"Boy's! What are you doing?" Mrs Summers roared in their direction.

Cameron quickly swivelled back around to face the front. Matthew *finally* blinked, and after a couple of deep breaths he managed to look up at his teacher.

"Nothing, Miss," Matthew answered calmly.

"Good, now where was I? Oh yes… " as Mrs Summers wittered on about different types of fiction and non-fiction books, Matthew rested his head in the palms of his hands and looked passively towards her.

For some unknown reason, images of Catherine, Crow and Camp Forgotten started to whizz around his head. He focussed firmly on Mrs Summers' mouth, trying hard to concentrate on what she was saying.

Then suddenly, like a dagger being thrust into the back of his hand, the cut which he had previously received from Clever Crow, started to beat. Swiftly he took his eyes away from Mrs Summers, distracted by the feeling of his veins pumping blood around his hand.

Not here, not now, Matthew thought to himself but no matter how hard he fought the throb, he was unable to stop it.

Everything around him appeared to slow down. Blocking out the classroom sound, he took his hand away from his face and placed it down onto the desk. Feeling completely dazed, he glanced up and switched his eyes frantically around the room. A chilling feeling overcame him, as he realised he was completely alone.

The classroom door was firmly closed and from underneath it a wispy layer of thinning fog crept. The fog climbed over the desks and chairs, slithering its way towards him.

Then from outside the window an ear piercing screech tore through the silence. It was the call that had haunted, tortured and tormented him over the past year. But now, now it was more real and clear than ever.

"Caw! Caw!" the call came again.

Matthew's heart raced rapidly inside his chest, sweat gathered in the palms of his hands, and small beads began to roll down his face.

Did he dare look? Was he *really* back?

He sat upright in his seat. The throbbing on the back of his hand had now become a faint ache as the call of Crow once more echoed around the empty classroom.

"Where are you?" Matthew asked in a whispered.

Slowly he turned his head and daringly looked out of the window.

And there *he* was.

Clever Crow had perched himself on top of one of the snow coated tree branches, relishing the fact that all the world could *watch* him, but only Matthew could *see* him. His tiny beady eyes stared down at Matthew.

Spreading wide his mighty, glorious wings, he stretched up onto the tips of his claws. Trustingly he leapt off the branch, letting the icy wind catch him, before freefalling towards the classroom window.

"No!" Matthew cried out, but it was too late.

The skin on his hand split open and an outburst of ruby red blood rushed. Crow swooped closer and closer, then purposefully lifting up his razor sharp claws, Crow smashed cleanly through the glass.

"No!" Matthew screamed jumping up from his seat.

"Mr Khan! That is it! I've had quite enough of you for one day. Collect your things and go straight to Mr Strokes' office!"

"What? But Miss, I… I… "

"No! I don't know what's gotten into you today, but I will not have my lesson disrupted anymore! Now go!" Mrs Summers gave her final orders to Matthew and pointed abruptly towards the classroom door.

As Matthew gathered up his stuff, Cassie looked up at him with a bewildered expression on her face, "Are you ok Matthew? You look pale."

"Yeah, yeah I'm fine. See you at dinner?" Matthew faintly asked.

"Maybe," Cassie replied quietly, shrugging her shoulders.

"Mr Khan!"

"I'm going!" Matthew answered.

"Good luck," Cassie whispered teasingly towards him, her cheeks flushing red.

"Thanks," Matthew replied, and with that he flung his bag over his shoulder and headed off out of the classroom in the direction of the head teacher's office.

Cassie slumped back in her chair and began to tap her pencil on the desk. She looked dagger eyed at Cameron Thomas. Somehow he had sensed her looking as on several occasions when Mrs Summers had turned away, he sharply twisted his neck and met her gaze.

Eventually the lesson was over and the dinner bell rang. Everyone, except Cassie, scraped their chairs back, packed away their books and pencil cases and headed off like a herd of cattle for dinner.

Cassie remained seated, thinking of Matthew. Should she go and see if he was waiting for her? Would Mr Strokes have finished giving him the third degree? She frowned and looked at his empty chair in front of her desk. Without another moment's hesitation, she threw all of her belongings into her denim shoulder bag and walked out of the classroom, leaving Mrs Summers marking books.

- Chapter Four -

Dinner Time Drama

"Cassie! Over here!" Amber's voice boomed over the crowded dinner hall.

Cassie glanced over towards the left hand side of the hall, and instantly a huge grin swept across her face. Her best friend, Amber, was frantically waving at her. However, Cassie's smile soon disappeared when she saw who was sat next to her, Sophia Green.

"Great," Cassie muttered to herself as she walked across the dinner hall towards them.

"Cass, come and sit here," Amber called over a little too excitedly as she patted the seat next to her. Sophia simply looked up, rolled her eyes and continued to eat her lunch.

"Thanks Amber," Cassie grinned through gritted teeth.

Amber and Cassie had been best friends since pre-school. They'd lived in Filius all of their lives, and although Amber didn't like Cassie spending so much

33

time with Matthew, she clung onto every little minute with Cassie that she could. Amber's bubbly personality and innocence was adorable. Her reddy brown curls bobbed around her small, round face. Freckles across her nose and cheeks further enhanced her pretty appearance. Amber's eyes were the colour of hazelnuts, unless she was sad then they were more black than brown. But today, as Cassie looked into Amber's smiling eyes, they were definitely hazelnut coloured.

Cassie sat herself down next to Amber and quickly glanced across at her worst nightmare, Sophia Green.

In appearance Sophia was the complete opposite to Amber. She was tall, slender and slim. Her long golden hair cascaded around her tanned tone face, over her shoulders and fell gracefully down her back. Sophia's most striking feature was her turquoise eyes which sparkled like jewels. She was determined to be the next best tennis player, with a great deal of encouragement from her father whom had been paying for private lessons since she was six. All the boys in Filius High, even the college boys, gave her attention. Unfortunately however, her personality didn't reflect her outer beauty. She was nasty and ruthless, and to quote Sophia's own words, *"I will stamp on anyone who gets in my way of success!"*

Sophia sensed Cassie's cold stare and sharply turned towards her, "So, where's your boyfriend then?"

"Matthew? He's *not* my boyfriend, we're just friends," Cassie replied crossly.

"Yeah right, I saw how you blushed in class earlier," Sophia remarked teasingly whilst pulling out a nail file from her bag.

"Come on Cassie, we're all girls here, you can tell us," Sophia pouted at Cassie, before frantically filing her nails.

Cassie raised her eyebrows, then turned away from Sophia and took out her lunch.

"Well?" Sophia asked, not letting the matter drop.

"Soph, we're *thirteen*, and to be honest we're just *good* friends!"

"Hmm… well, if you don't think he's boyfriend material maybe I –" Sophia began.

"No!" Cassie bellowed out, unfortunately a bit louder than she'd wished. "What I meant," she continued, this time lowering her voice to a whisper, "he's got *issues*."

Sophia suddenly stopped the nail file in mid thrust and looked intriguingly across at Cassie, "He's not still on about that stupid bird and Catherine Rose, is he?" both Amber and Sophia leant closer towards Cassie, their eyes growing wide with suspense.

"Don't say anything, please," Cassie pleaded. They both motioned a cross over their hearts. "Ok, well, this morning he actually called me Catherine."

"No!" gasped Sophia and Amber.

"I know!" Cassie nodded in agreement to their shocked gasps.

"Well, what did you say?" Amber asked.

"Nothing, I just, well you know, ignored it," Cassie replied in a sheepish manner.

"You did what? Cassie!" Amber returned. Her voice once more boomed over the dinner hall chatter, causing a few of the people on the other tables to turn and look towards the three girls.

Cassie darted Amber a killer look, "Sorry," Amber whispered.

"Anyway, I'm going to just give him a wide berth, I think," Cassie said trying to convince herself of her own words.

"Yeah right, a wide berth, more like a wide kiss! It's so obvious you fancy him –" Sophia said sarcastically.

"I don't –" Cassie stated unconvincingly.

"Cassie, I'm your best friend and even I can tell you're into him, and before you start the whole, *I'm only thirteen* excuse, don't, it doesn't work on me." And with that Amber sat back in her chair and folded her arms tightly across her chest.

Cassie sat quietly back in her chair too, knowing that no matter what she said, Amber wouldn't believe her. Cassie then slowly tucked into her sandwich, nibbling tiny pieces. Taking out her carton of orange juice she sipped it slowly. All the while she thought of Matthew.

"Hey look who's heading in our direction?" Sophia said, poking her elbow into Amber's side.

Marching his way across the dinner hall, followed by his little pack of groupies, was Cameron. His baseball cap sat sideways on his head, and his school pants were way too low, revealing his *Bart Simpson* yellow boxer shorts.

"Great," the three girls sighed in unison.

"What's up?" Cameron called towards them, revealing his crooked teeth as he grinned.

"Excuse me," Sophia replied in her put on posh voice.

"I said, what's up ladies?" Cameron grinned again.

"Not your pants for one thing!" Amber chuckled, causing Cassie to laugh too.

His white complexion turned a deep shade of pale red, and looking down at his pants, he quickly pulled them up over his boxers.

"What d'ya want, Cam?" Cassie huffed.

"Where's your boyf?" Cameron asked tilting his head back. His pack of tiny followers all sniggered around him.

"My what?" Cassie asked trying not to burst out laughing at Cameron attempt to be cool using slang terms.

"You know your b-o-y-f-r-i-e-n-d?" Cameron asked slowly.

"I don't know, not that it's any of your business, *but Matthew is not my boyfriend*!" Cassie shouted the last bit of her sentence just so everyone could hear her. She could now feel herself getting flustered. Throwing her half eaten sandwich back into her bag, she stood up to face Cameron.

"You know Cameron, you really are a loser. What with your baseball cap that clearly doesn't fit your oversized head, your bright yellow boxer shorts on display which shout out: '*Hey look at how big my backside is.*' And your little groupies who like nodding dogs hang onto your every word," Cassie said addressing his little tribe then continued, "just to make this perfectly clear, what I do with Matthew is my business, not yours, and not anyone else's!"

Cassie glanced down at Amber and Sophia, whose jaws were hung open in total shock at Cassie's outburst. Stunned, Cameron coughed a couple of times, bowed his head towards the door and swiftly walked off with his tribe of followers in close pursuit. Cassie could feel her eyes filling with tears and without saying another word, she too headed off out through the dinner hall and exited into a snow covered playground.

Cassie stood for a moment. Gathering her thoughts,

and her breath, she set off past the outside of Mr Strokes' office window. At that moment she was startled to see that Matthew was standing in the head teacher's office. Upon seeing her he smiled that warming smile she loved, and then he lifted his hand to wave. Cassie didn't respond but simply turned away and set off back towards the school.

As she turned a corner, a gust of wind blew up into her face. She instantly put her hands up in front of her to shield her face from the icy breeze. Then she felt something whip against her leg, she looked down and noticed that wrapped around her ankle was a tatty piece of paper. She bent over to pull it off but the wind blew stronger against her, preventing her removing it. Lowering her head, she shoved open one of the doors and swiftly moved back into the safety of school. The wintery wind whirred behind her, causing the door to slam shut.

Although relieved to be back in the warmth, Cassie noticed that the school seemed unusually quiet. To the left of her was the girls' cloakroom and without a second thought, Cassie went in.

"Look at the state of me," she said to her reflection in the mirror.

Unzipping her bag, she pulled out a hair brush and began to tug through her ruffled, windswept hair. Then in the corner of her eye she saw something move, a shadow of some sort. She frowned and shook her head, then she continued to brush.

There it was again; a black outline reflected in the bottom corner of the mirror. She focussed her eyes on the mirror willing it to reappear. Her body started to tremble with the fear of whom or what it could be.

She watched and waited. Then, there it was.

She quickly turned about on the heel of her foot, and standing next to the toilet door only a few inches away from her, was a black crow.

A first it startled her but then as it remained motionless, seemingly more scared of her then she was of it, she reached out to touch its silky soft coat.

The crow didn't move its beady eyes off Cassie's face. Welcoming her warm touch upon its feathers, *this* crow was pleased to be this close to Matthew's *new* friend.

Noticing the entangled piece of paper still wrapped around Cassie's ankle, the crow hopped forward towards her. Then pointing its beak down onto the floor, Cassie noticed the paper too.

"Oh, I thought that would have blown off," Cassie muttered.

With one motion, Cassie pulled the paper off from the bottom of her tights and turned it over to reveal a picture printed on the front. At first Cassie dismissed it but then upon a closer second glance, she began to shake.

Gripping it tight with both her hands, she stood upright and glared down at the gloss shiny paper which somehow seemed to glare back at her.

"Oh my… " she gasped.

It was Catherine.

It wasn't the same as all the other leaflets. There were no details about her disappearance, just a picture of her behind some old, rusty bars. She was sat hunched over on the floor with her arms locked together and was looking directly forward. Her once red hair was washed free of colour, her body resembled a skeleton, and her face was long and gaunt. But her eyes, her eyes stood out, almost crying out for help, tear filled and lost. And the most haunting thing of all, written across the bottom in blue biro were two words… *help me*.

"Where are you, Catherine?" Cassie called looking down at the picture in bewilderment.

Mesmerised by the picture, Cassie walked out of the cloakroom to a now bustling school corridor.

The bell had just sounded, and the children rushed up and down the corridor going to their classes. Cassie, in a world of her own, wandered along too, her eyes transfixed upon the picture. Cassie couldn't feel the kids pushing by her; first knocking her one way then the other.

Suddenly, a heavy hand grabbed her shoulder and twirled her around.

41

Instantly Cassie looked up. Standing in front of her, his olive skin aglow under the dingy school lights, smiling down towards her, was Matthew. Her mouth went dry, and her throat felt as though someone had tightly gripped it. Unable to control her emotions, her eyes flooded with tears.

"Cass, what is it? Are you ok?" Matthew asked grabbing her with both his hands. "Cassie!"

Matthew looked down at the piece of paper which Cassie was holding. Releasing his grip on her, he took hold of the paper and forcefully pulled it out of Cassie's tight grip.

"Catherine," he muttered as his eyes fell upon her face. Seeing her brought it all back, causing the memories of Darkmoor to come to the forefront of his mind. The cut on his hand pounded as fast as his heart beat.

"Catherine… Cassie where did you get this? Cassie, tell me!" Matthew's voice rose with intensity, his eyes filled with pain.

"Tell me!" he demanded again.

"The…the…cloakroom. I was in the girl's cloakroom and the – " Cassie replied, her voice trailing off.

"Tell me Cassie, what did you see?"

"A crow, Matthew, there was a crow."

Immediately Matthew headed off down the corridor, pushing his way past all the children before forcefully slamming open the girl's cloakroom door. The noise of giggly girls' filtered out.

"Get out!" one of the girls' shrieked towards him.

"Sorry, have any of you seen a crow? A black crow?" Matthew frantically asked.

"Nope!" another girl laughed before the whole cloakroom erupted with laughter too.

"Are you… it's just my friend saw one earlier and – " Matthew began.

"Get out!" a chorus of girls' screamed at him.

"Yeah sorry," Matthew said casually trying to regain some dignity.

Matthew started to walk back down the corridor and headed straight for Cassie. She was still stood in the same spot, completely white, jaw dropped and looking out for Matthew.

Seeing Cameron heading down the corridor towards Cassie, Matthew quickly scrunched up the piece of paper and shoved it firmly into his pant pocket.

Unfortunately, Cameron got to Cassie first, and taking advantage of her daydreaming state, he put his arms around her shoulders.

"You ok babe?" he asked her, all the while watching Matthew.

"Yeah, yeah I'm good thanks," Cassie replied vacantly.

"Cassie," Matthew called over. Upon hearing his voice she shuffled out from under Cameron's arm and looked up at Matthew.

"Oh come on Cassie babe, you can't honestly prefer bird boy to me?" Cameron teased obnoxiously.

She didn't answer him but rather walked towards Matthew.

"Are you ok?" Matthew asked caringly, her face was still as white as snow.

Without a word, she just nodded and smiled at him.

"Hey, bird boy!" Cameron called.

Matthew was about to turn and look at him, but Cassie reached out and grabbed his hand.

"Don't… " she pleaded, "… he's not worth it."

"I think we've got some unfinished business, don't you? Or are you chicken?" Cameron's tribe of groupies made clucking noises, much to Cameron's approval.

"No hang on…it's not chickens you're afraid of but… " Cameron lowered his voice to a whisper but even then, over the noise of the school, Matthew heard him say, "… crows."

Cameron's followers stopped clucking and instead started cawing, all the while running around Cameron flapping their arms like wings.

Matthew suddenly stopped dead. His face seemed to narrow, and his eyes turned black. He squeezed Cassie's hand tight and could feel his heart almost jumping out of his chest. Then before his eyes flashed the man of his nightmares, Darkmoor. Rage overcame him and a deep anger welled up from within. He looked down at Cassie, who was shaking her head at him, telling him to leave it. But that's all he'd ever done, *just left it*. He'd ignored the teasing over and over again. He'd learnt to bury all those emotions, all those memories, but not now, not anymore.

Releasing Cassie's hand, Matthew turned to face Cameron. Everybody close by fell silent, and Matthew fixed his cold steely eyes upon Cameron Thomas.

"What – did – you – say?" Matthew slowly asked in a chilling voice. Cassie stepped away from him unable to fully recognise the boy that stood before her.

"You heard me, bird boy!" Cameron smirked whilst winking at Cassie.

"Fight! Fight! Fight!" the chanting started from a huge crowd that had gathered around Matthew and Cameron.

"No Matthew!" Cassie called but her voice was muffled over the chants.

Both boys eyed each other up. Matthew was slightly taller than Cameron, but Cameron held more weight.

"I'm gonna enjoy this," Cameron whispered.

"Me too," Matthew replied in an icy voice.

Cassie ran off screaming down the hall. The crowd cheered, and the horrible sound of skin against skin echoing along the corridor. Quickly she reached the head teacher's office, and without knocking she burst in.

"Cassie, what are you doing?" Mr Strokes asked looking up from his computer.

"It's Cameron and Matthew –" she panted pointing down the corridor. Upon hearing the chanting, Mr Strokes jumped up from his chair and marched off down towards the huge crowd of children.

"That's enough!" Mr Strokes boomed. Instantly the onlookers retreated and made their way back down the halls, leaving behind Cameron and Matthew.

"What do you think you're doing? Both of you… my office… now!"

Both boys looked at each other, wiped the blood away from the noses, grabbed their bags and followed behind Mr Strokes.

Cassie stood out of their way, and as Matthew passed by her, she saw his eyes had now changed back to their natural sky blue colour. He smiled up at her and continued to walk in a care free manner behind Mr Strokes.

- Chapter Five -

Daring To Believe

"But please Mr McKendry, can I talk to him, just for a moment," Cassie pleaded as she stood on the door step of the old vicarage.

"I'm sorry Cassie love, he's grounded," Jack replied firmly.

With batting eyelids, Cassie looked up, "Please, it's *really* important."

Jack let out a sigh, a small smile appeared in the corner of his mouth, "Ok, but ten minutes, that's all!"

"Thanks, Mr McKendry!" Cassie called cheerfully before skipping past Jack down the hallway towards the kitchen.

Matthew was sat at the breakfast table doing some *extra* homework that he and Cameron had been given. Seeing Cassie appear in the doorway instantly brought a smile to his face. "What you doing here?" Matthew asked.

"Your dad said I could see you for ten minutes," replied Cassie with a smile.

"Yes and I mean ten minutes Matthew!" Jack shouted through from the sitting room.

"Quick, close the door... he always listens in," Matthew said lowering his voice.

Slowly and carefully Cassie pushed the door shut, and then jumped up onto a stool before leaning closer towards Matthew.

Completely misreading the situation, Matthew leaned in too and went to kiss her.

"What are you doing?" Cassie asked confused whilst quickly pulling herself away from his puffed up lips.

"Sorry I thought you, you know, wanted a kiss," Matthew grinned whilst stroking his fingers through his hair.

Cassie blushed and giggled, "No, I'm good thanks. *Anyway*, have you got that piece of paper, you know the one with Catherine on?"

"Yeah why?" Matthew asked puzzled.

"Cause I want to have another look at it," Cassie demanded putting her hand out in front of her.

"I don't think so Cass," Matthew replied shaking his head. "You don't know what you're getting yourself into, I mean... "

"Matthew, please, look you and me both know humans can't change into crow's but one thing we do know is Catherine is still missing and that –"

"Cassie, you really don't know anything. I'll keep the piece of paper and sort it, ok!" Matthew's abrupt voice caught Cassie off guard.

"What d'ya mean *you'll sort it*?" Cassie paused for a moment before continuing, "Matthew, do you know where she is?"

Matthew picked up his pencil and turned his attention back to his *extra* homework. Looking up towards Cassie, he muttered sternly, "You can go now."

"Go? I'm not going anywhere! Tell me where she is Matthew!"

Matthew quickly reached across the breakfast bar, and putting his hand over Cassie's mouth he reminded her that Jack was in the next room.

"I already have, but no one believed me, *remember*?" Matthew said, slowly taking his hand away.

"You mean, Dark… "

"Darkmoor, yes… yes Cassie."

"But you said, you told everyone…" Cassie stuttered.

"You said it was all a dream and that you'd made it all up. Why? Why would you do that?" Cassie looked directly at Matthew. Her face flushing red with anguish, her eyes filled with anger as she waited for an answer which actually made some sense.

"I know it sounds crazy and it probably is, but the

truth is, Darkmoor does exist. Everything I said last year is true, the car boot sale, the old man, the snow globe… "

"No! No it can't be, come on Matthew, this is me, you can tell me the truth," Cassie whispered reaching her hand across the breakfast bar and placing it on top of his.

Matthew quickly slid his hand away from her, his eyes glazing over like ice towards her, "I am telling you the truth! Why don't you believe me?"

"Because, come on Matthew, these places aren't real… you know that, right?"

"Don't patronise me, Cassie!"

"I'm not, it's just, it's a lot to take in, that's all," Cassie muttered shaking her head.

Matthew felt agitated by Cassie's comment and started marching around the kitchen. Then he suddenly stopped and slowly turned around.

"How can you say you don't believe me Cassie? You've seen him, Crow, the picture… " Matthew began frantically searching in his pants pocket. Eventually he pulled out the scrunched up picture of Catherine.

Slamming it down on the bar, he moved the palm of his hand to smooth out the creases.

Matthew looked up at Cassie. Her eyes twitched about the kitchen trying desperately to make sense of it all. She had *never* believed any of it before but after today's events, with the crow, the picture of Catherine…

"Look Cassie, look at her. She's trapped there. How can you *not* believe me?" Matthew softly spoke, his voice sounding broken.

Cassie didn't say a word. She just sat there staring down at the photo of Catherine, longing to believe Matthew, but how?

"I swear, I'm not making it up Cass," Matthew whispered faintly, breaking the deafening silence which had settled in the kitchen.

Slowly Cassie placed her hand back on top of his, only this time he wasn't so quick to move it away. Squeezing his hand tight, she whispered, "I believe you."

At that moment a sense of relief washed over Matthew. At last those words he'd longed to hear. A big smile stretched across his face, looking up from the picture of Catherine, Matthew hesitantly asked, "Really?"

Cassie looked up at him with tear filled eyes but still she managed a smile. Gently she replied, "Yes, I have to admit at first I did think you were a lunatic, but now… " Cassie's voice trailed off as her eyes fell once again upon Catherine's face, "… look at her Matthew. We have to do something… "

"I know Cass, and believe me I've been trying but there's just… " Matthew suddenly stopped talking. His eyes glazed over as if he was daydreaming.

"What Matthew?"

"You, you saw him today... that's it, it all makes sense now," Matthew began to march back around the kitchen. "Don't you see Cassie, he's back."

Cassie shook her head trying to catch up with Matthew's thoughts, "Who?"

"Crow of course! Nothing for a whole year, no signs, no hints of him returning, but then this morning Dad was reading the paper and the headline read: *Crow is back –*"

"Darren Crow the footballer?" Cassie asked still slightly confused.

"Yeah, but why would my dad tell me that? He doesn't even like football."

"Ok," Cassie muttered slowly.

"Then this morning, before you turned up, I heard him, cawing... " Matthew turned away from Cassie. Running his fingers through his hair, he darted his eyes all over the kitchen, all the while mumbling continually under his breath.

Cassie watched on as Matthew marched back and forth. Once more her eyes fell on Catherine. She picked up the paper, rubbed her thumb across Catherine's image and whispered, "Oh Catherine."

Suddenly the kitchen door burst open startling them both. Cassie almost fell off her stool and Matthew came to a halt. Quickly Cassie folded the paper up and shoved it into her jacket pocket.

"Mr McKendry," Cassie said swivelling round on the stool. "You gave us a fright."

"Sorry Cassie love, but I did say ten minutes and by my clock," Jack stopped and tapped the face of his wrist watch.

"Come on Dad, we're not doing anything wrong, can she just stay for a bit longer?" Matthew pleaded.

"Matthew, when I say you're grounded, you're grounded! I've let her see you, don't push it Son." Jack firmly folded his arms across his chest and raised his eyebrows across the kitchen towards Matthew.

Cassie jumped off her stool, causing it to spin as she left the seat. She smiled warmly towards Matthew, "I'll see you at school tomorrow, Matt," she said swiftly brushing past Jack, who stood tall in the doorway.

Hearing the latch click on the front door, Matthew sighed, "Thanks, Dad."

"Fighting at school Matthew is not something I take lightly. What were you thinking? Anyway, if we don't get a move on, you're gonna be late for Doctor Wicks," Jack said with a wicked smile upon his lips, "and I know how much you enjoy your visits," he added teasingly exiting the kitchen.

"Yeah, right," Matthew replied unimpressed.

"Come on, you remember what he said last week?"

"Yeah I know," Matthew smiled half heartedly at Jack. Stepping back towards the breakfast bar, he picked up his jacket and followed on behind.

Jack swiftly grabbed the car keys from the sideboard. He looked over his shoulder and winked at Matthew, "So, Cassie then, she's pretty –"

"Shut up, Dad!" Matthew smirked, pushing his dad out of the front door and into the snow.

- Chapter Six -

Camp Life

Unaware of Matthew's movements and the fact that he and Catherine were still alive, and that Sam had indeed tricked them all time and time again, Camp Forgotten gathered around the burning fire, ready to eat another grizzly, fat, wolf-lizard.

Time had moved on in here to. Every one of the campers had grown up, and even the two young ones, Thomas and Isabella, had learnt to survive the misery of camp life.

With every day that passed, the memories of Matthew, Catherine and Sam faded, so too did the hope of them returning with good news.

However camp remained the same. Five mud hut shelters situated in a horse shoe shape around the camp fire. The two towering pillars burnt bright in the gloomy grey sky, and the warm, welcoming fire crackled joyfully with each new piece of wood.

The skinned beast, which was from the days' earlier

catch, had been skewered like a hog roast and dangled over the hot ashes. Bloody juices sweated out of the wolf-lizards body as the campers eagerly waited for the juices to flow clear, so they could eat their familiar dinner.

"Wash your hands, it's nearly ready," Reuben spoke up.

Instantly the campers stood up and rushed over to the barrel of rain water. One by one they dipped their hands into the rusty barrel and shook them to dry.

"Reuben?" Isabella asked wearily. "Can we have something else to eat tomorrow?"

Reuben looked up from the fire and smiled down at Isabella. A half smile appeared on her charcoal smeared face, and despite the absence of her once rosy cheeks, her piercing blue eyes still emitted a message of innocence.

"Issy… " Reuben replied softly, not wanting to upset her, "… I'll see what I can do."

A huge smile lit up her face. "Yeah!" she shouted jumping up and down before him. She opened her arms wide and flung herself towards him, "Thank you Reuben, thank you!"

"Isabella," Jasmine teasingly called from behind her. "Leave Reuben alone and go wash your hands and *face* for dinner."

"Ok, Jasmine," Isabella replied joyfully, pulling away from Reuben's warm hug. She skipped past Jasmine and smiled before skipping over to the others. She then called back, "Love you Reuben."

Jasmine watched her for a few moments; *the angel of the camp*. Isabella always brought a smile to your face, her innocence was adorable, and even now over a year on, she wasn't frightened of the surroundings that she'd involuntarily found herself in.

Jasmine turned to look at Reuben, who was also watching Isabella, "I think you've got an admirer there," Jasmine smiled raising her eyebrows.

"Feeling threatened Jas?" Reuben fired back.

"No, no," Jasmine stuttered, her face blushing bright red.

Reuben chuckled, "Don't worry, I'm only interested in the *older* women!" he said with a smirk and a wink.

Jasmine quickly bowed her head allowing her long black her to hide her embarrassed face. Reuben chuckled again then he started to carve the beast with a knife.

Jasmine slowly brushed her hair to one side and looked back at him. She couldn't help but watch as he masterfully motioned the knife under the skin of the wolf-lizard. Effortlessly he sliced pink slithers of meat from the beast and placed them into a wooden dish. She found herself breathless, wondering at what point during this whole nightmare had Reuben grown from a boy into a man, the man which she had fallen in love with. She was unclear of his feelings towards her, and she'd never confessed her love for him, only Claire knew how she felt. At first she tried to stop it, run from it, make herself believe it wasn't true, but over time as her and Reuben spent more time together, she realised she'd fallen more in love with him.

"Jas… Jas… Earth to Jasmine," Reuben's voice drifted towards her. He waved his hand in front of her face trying to break her stare.

"Jasmine!"

She blinked several times then she coughed to clear her throat, "Sorry, I was miles away," she said smiling nervously, looking away from him.

"What were you thinking about?" Reuben asked.

"Erm…I was thinking about…you know… " Jasmine spluttered.

"Go on," Reuben coaxed.

"Never mind, is dinner ready?" Jasmine smirked towards him. He smiled back at her in return, and without another word she started passing around the dishes of meat.

Once dinner was over, Claude, Olli and Thomas started to wash the pots, leaving Andrew and Reuben to unhook the skewered beast. Leaving camp to discard of its skeleton remains, Nathan decided to go with them in the hope of bringing back some fresh logs for the fire.

Claire sat down on a stump whilst Isabella sat down on the floor in front of her. Pressing herself up against Claire's legs, Isabella rested her head upon her lap. Claire gently combed her fingers through her knotted curly hair.

"What do you think, Jas?" Claire asked looking up at Jasmine, who sat opposite them.

"Hmm?" Jasmine muffled.

"You know…about leaving camp?" Claire whispered in the hope that Isabella wouldn't hear.

"I don't know," Jasmine replied in an agitated manner.

"Jasmine!" Claire shouted across at her.

"Shush, Claire," Jasmine sharply said raising her eyebrows back at Claire.

Claire looked down at Isabella, "Oh sorry," she said, suddenly remembering that little ears *might* be listening in.

Isabella looked up, her eyes wide, "What is it Claire?"

"Nothing sweet-pea," Claire said softly patting the top of Isabella's head. "Why don't you go and help the boys wash up?"

Isabella pouted her lips then shifting her eyes from Claire to Jasmine, then back again to Claire, stood up, huffed a few times before stomping off towards her brother Thomas, and Olli, who appeared to have become bored with washing up and had started a water fight.

"Boys!" Claire shouted at them only to be answered

by a chorus of giggles.

Jasmine smiled and shook her head, "What are they like?"

"So? When are you going to tell Reuben about… you know," Claire said quietly leaning forward on her stump.

"What?" Jasmine replied innocently, "Tell him what?"

"Oh, come on Jas, you know what I mean, tell him how you feel."

"No way," Jasmine said throwing a couple of twigs on the roaring fire. "Now's really not the right time. Not with them talking about leaving camp."

"Of course it is. Jasmine, that's all the more reason to tell him," Claire stated.

"Oh, yeah, right. Reuben, you know how we're about to go, leave camp and maybe get killed, well, just before we do I've got something to tell you –"

A chorus of voices singing merrily accompanied the heavy gates being forced open. In the light of the fire Andrew, Nathan and Reuben appeared, each holding a bundle of wood.

"It's ok ladies," Andrew shouted over sarcastically, "we can manage!"

"Oh!" Claire called, then turning back towards Jasmine she quietly muttered, "This conversation is not over."

"Here you go bro," Claude said to Reuben, offering to help with his load.

"Thanks," Reuben said unloading some of his logs onto Claude. Turning to look down at Isabella, a crooked smirk tickled his lips, "What have you been up to? You're wet through!"

Isabella's hair was dripping wet, Olli was laughing at Thomas, and Thomas was holding a dish full of water which was aimed and ready to fire at Isabella.

"Ok you three," Jasmine spoke. "That's quite enough. I think it's bedtime for Issy and Tom."

"Oh," whined Thomas and Isabella.

"Nevermind that, come on!" Jasmine said assertively sounding more like a mum.

Thomas slowly poured the dish full of water onto the muddy floor and sulked off into his mud hut. Isabella stuck out her tongue and blew a raspberry as she walked past Jasmine.

Dragging his feet, Thomas opened the door to his hut, took off his wet clothes and climbed into his bed.

"Good night, Issy."

"Good night, Tom."

- Chapter Seven -

Planning Their Fate

"No, Nathan! If we do this *we all* do this!" Andrew asserted.

"You're crazy Andrew, that's not an option," Nathan boomed over the crackling fire.

"Andrew *has* got a point though, Nath," Claire joined in.

"No, no, no!" Nathan stated in a calm and collected manner, "Isabella, Thomas and Olli, they're all far too young."

"What do you want us to do? Leave them here on their own? I agree with Andrew, if we do this *we all* do this," Reuben commented looking up at Nathan. Nathan circled the fire like a lion hunting prey: fierce, fiery and frightening.

There was a few moments silence. Orange, amber and yellow flames soared up into the darkened sky. Everybody sat staring at tiny fireflies dancing in and out of the mesmerising flames, pondering the thought of going across the River of Souls and entering the unknown.

Nathan finally settled back down on his stump. Resting his chin on his rough, worn palms, he sighed heavily.

Claire sat down next to him, her eyes softly falling upon his frowning face, "Nathan, you know it makes sense. We have to all go across, Isabella, Tom, Olli, all of us." She reached out and placed her hand upon his shoulder. Heavily, he lifted his head up from his hands and looked at her.

"Do you really think we can do this?" Nathan whispered with a hint of desperation in his voice.

Claire threw a half hearted smile towards him before whispering back, "I don't think we have a choice."

Nathan slowly nodded his head before looking up through the flames of the fire to meet Andrews's gaze.

"You're right, if we do this we all go together," Nathan declared powerfully to the group whilst trying to convince himself it was the right decision.

Everyone, except for Jasmine, nodded. Jasmine leant forward on her stump and stared at the ground, her eyes filling up as she gulped several times.

"You ok Jas?" Reuben asked shuffling towards her.

Without looking, she simply nodded. Reuben placed a hand on her back.

"Right then, decision made!" Nathan jumped up energetically to his feet, all his doubt had seemingly disappeared. "This is it. Tomorrow we'll start getting all of the things we'll need," Nathan looked across at Andrew, "one week?"

"Yeah, one week should be plenty," Andrew replied rubbing his overgrown beard.

"Good, then Camp Forgotten, it's time to fight back!" Nathan called out in a patriotic voice through gritted teeth. Then swiftly he turned and set off towards his hut.

"Better start planning, I guess," Andrew muttered under his breath before strolling off towards his hut too.

Jasmine looked up and half smiled at Reuben, "Guess this is it then."

"Yep, guess so," Reuben replied in a matter of fact manner.

Jasmine's heart sank in her chest. Slowly she turned away from him as tiny tears rolled down her cheeks. Not wanting him to see, Jasmine stood up and began to walk aimlessly across the camp.

Sensing Claire's gaze, Reuben looked up.

"What?" Reuben asked innocently, shrugging his shoulders and throwing her a crooked grin.

"Do you know, Reuben, sometimes… oh I give up," Claire sighed as she threw her hands up into the air.

Then following the others, she too marched off across the camp and disappeared into one of the huts.

This left Reuben, who sat on his own, carefully poking the logs, ensuring the fire wouldn't die. He thought about the others, all of them, his brothers, Andrew and Nathan, Issy and Tom, Claire and Jasmine.

'Is Jasmine mad at me?' he thought, re-thinking over the whole day, trying to recall anything he might have done that would have upset her, but he couldn't think of anything. He looked over his shoulder and positioned directly behind him was the shelter into which Jasmine had disappeared.

'Should I go and see if she's ok?' he pondered for a moment. Slowly, he pushed himself up but then quickly sat down again on his stump.

"Girls," he muttered, throwing some more wood onto the fire.

High up above flapping his wings slowly up and down, was Crow. He had been listening to every little word whispered. Revenge flooded his piercing black beady eyes. He smirked to himself as they *pathetically* believed they could somehow defeat him. He watched intently for a moment longer then as graceful as ever, he flew back over to his side of Darkmoor.

Instantly, as his claws touched the hard ground below, his animal body transformed back into its human state. Across his gaunt drawn out face appeared his wicked grin. Using his long skeleton fingers he pulled out a black feather from the back of his throat and released it. Like a spinning jenny, the freed feather spiralled down into the mud below.

"That's better," he grimaced.

He trotted off up towards his castle with his black overcoat swaying from side to side. Then stopping still on the top step, just like he'd done every time, Darkmoor turned back around and looked masterfully down over his creation, his land, his kingdom. Then lifting his hands up into the dark sky above, bellowed out a roar of laughter.

"Let them come and fight me!" he called. His voice echoed around the castle walls and rumbled off down into the graveyard below.

"I will just simply have to kill them all," he spoke full of delight. His eyes lit up with joy in anticipation of the battle *they'd* been planning.

"Oh, Catherine!" he suddenly remembered, turning back around. He marched up the alleyway and into the Roman theatre. Logan stood there waiting for his master to return.

Logan was only a boy. Not much older than eleven years old, but after living here with Darkmoor most of his life, he regarded himself more of a man than a boy. He copied every move that Darkmoor made and took great pleasure in pleasing his master. He wasn't as tall or slim as Darkmoor, quite the opposite, he was short and stocky. Burnt amber eyes sunk deep into Logan's pale round face with golden hair that hung rugged down upon his shoulders. His voice was soft and smooth yet slightly high pitched. But behind that innocent appearance of Logan there laid a darker side. Logan was Darkmoor's son. He had witnessed the killings, the tortures, and the hunting's. He'd watched on in the wings of the theatre, as Darkmoor had ordered his monsters to kill Catherine. Furthermore, it was him who had turned the lock on Catherine's cell, and then repeatedly teased and tormented her. Yes, he might not physically look like his master, but as far as he was concerned, Darkmoor *was* his father.

"Son, there you are!" Darkmoor called.

"Father," Logan muttered and ran across the theatre towards Darkmoor.

Holding Logan at arm's length, Darkmoor looked down into his eyes, "Have you fed Catherine today?" he asked.

Shamefully Logan lowered his head, "Sorry Father… " Logan stuttered nervously.

"Son, I give you one thing to do and you can't even do that," Darkmoor said shaking his head in disappointment. "Please tell me Dove is *still* in her cage?"

"Yes, Father," Logan said faintly as he looked away from his father's stare.

"Thank goodness for that, you're not completely incapable then? You'd better go and get our guest. I've got some news for her."

"What, you mean *unlock* her?" Logan asked surprised.

"Yes boy!" Darkmoor's voice boomed. "That's what I mean, she can eat with us tonight... " Darkmoor's voice faded as he stepped past Logan then swiftly turned, "...Do you think you can do that?" Darkmoor smirked towards Logan. Without waiting for him to answer, Darkmoor marched off into the darkness of the theatre and slammed the dining room door to.

"Of course I can," Logan whispered sarcastically to himself. Taking a deep breath in, he made his way towards the archway which lead down into the dungeon.

Logan grabbed hold of a burning torch causing the light to flicker as his hands shook. He'd taken Catherine bread and water every day, well almost every day. He would often check up on her when Darkmoor had taken to the skies, but never, never had he unlocked her cell door and invited her to eat with them.

Breathing heavily, he paused for a moment on the top step. Then as if she had been awaiting his visit, Catherine let out a faint cry from the dark pit below.

"Logan... Logan? Is that you?"

At first he didn't answer, for he didn't want her to hear the trembling nervousness in his voice.

"Logan… " her soft delicate voice called again.

He closed his eyes tight trying to block out her call, trying to picture his father's stern, cold, gaunt face instead. Squeezing them tighter, suddenly there it was. The look of disappointment on Darkmoor's face, the look that made Logan feel completely worthless, unloved and lost. The more he pictured his father's dark, soulless eyes looking into his, the more like Darkmoor he became. Instead of the shame and pity that he felt whenever he heard Catherine's voice, now he was beginning to feel nothing but revenge and anger.

Instantly Logan's eyes shot open. His hands were no longer shaking, confidently he set foot onto the stairwell. Lifting the burning torch out in front of him, he called down to Catherine.

"Yes Catherine, it's me," his voice no longer resembled that of the nervous wreck he was previously. It was now cold and steely, sounding just like his father's.

- Chapter Eight -

Catherine's Innocence Exposed

"Catherine my dear, please come in," Darkmoor spoke raising his arms to greet her with an unwelcome, evil smirk across his face.

Logan gave her a firm shove from behind, causing Catherine to stumble into the dining room.

The glow of candlelight lit up Catherine's face, and bowing her head down towards the floor her scraggy hair to fall about her face.

Darkmoor pouted his lips, "Catherine, Catherine," his voice sent a shiver down her spine. He skipped towards her, and placing his hand underneath her chin he forcefully lifted up her face to look at him.

"That's better, now we can see each other," he smiled.

She tried to pull herself away from his grip but the more she tried, the tighter his grip became.

"Now, now Catherine, there's no need for that. I thought you'd like to join us for dinner," he held her in place for a few more moments then slowly released his grip, leaving a red mark upon her washed out skin.

"Come, let's sit down and eat," Darkmoor said gesturing towards the thick, worn, wooden table that stood in the centre of the room, surrounded by six tall wooden chairs with each one decorated with twigs. In a straight line down the middle of the table, crumpled up brown leaves had been scattered, and at each place setting sat six small round wooden bowls ready for dinner.

Dotted randomly on the stone walls where silver candle holders. A mixture of red and white tall candles sat within them franticly flickering. Wooden beams stretched from wall to wall across the ceiling, each one alight with candles. The main feature of the room however wasn't the candles light or the solid oak table, or the chunky wooden beams, but the huge open fire which sunk deep into the back wall of the dining room. Freely the fire burnt as it warmed up its surroundings. Catherine watched as the flames danced together, and she couldn't help but think of camp. For just like the camps fire, this open fire had a wolf-lizard spit roast draped over too.

Catherine watched on as the flames furiously wrapped themselves around the beast. She felt her eyes filling with tears, desperately longing to be as free as the flames themselves. Determined however not to show

Darkmoor any sign of her weakness, Catherine blinked several times then she turned away from the fire.

Darkmoor trotted up towards the beasty dinner, and once again Logan pushed Catherine from behind. She turned angrily to face him but ignoring her he simply walked past and took his place at the table.

Noticing that the door was still slightly ajar, Catherine thought about turning and dashing through it. Darkmoor had his back turned, and Logan was too busy watching his father prod and poke their feast. Slowly she shuffled back, and step by step she moved closer towards the open door, but then she stopped. She looked first at Darkmoor then her eyes looked towards Logan. Something inside of her pained. An emotion she'd never expected… sympathy? Surely not!

She turned to face the door once more, but yet again something stopped her.

Darkmoor was her living nightmare, he'd tortured her, laughed at her, had kept her locked away for over a year, but still she didn't fear him. And Logan, every day he brought her bread and water and made nasty remarks. He tried to play the bad guy but there was something deep inside him that set him apart from Darkmoor. It was like he was fighting with himself every day, but nevertheless, he was only a boy trying to please his father.

Again Catherine shuffled towards the door but that churning of emotion finally got the better of her. Half heartedly she trudged to the table, and quietly she sat herself down opposite Logan.

She didn't look up at him, but she sensed he was staring at her.

"Well, isn't this nice," Darkmoor spoke up, picking up the carving knife from the table.

"The *boy* who longs to be like his father, and the *girl* who fell in love with a crow!"

Catherine looked up sharply, "What?" her voice was faint, but then coughing to clear her throat she asked again, "what did you say?"

"Now, now dear don't be mad, but did you really think I wouldn't read your diary?"

"You… you had *no* right!" Catherine screamed.

Darkmoor shot around the table, and he stood behind Catherine. Kneeling down besides her he whispered, "Oh I know I shouldn't have, but as it was mostly about me, I couldn't help but read on."

Catherine could feel his icy breath on the back of her neck. His eyes were burning into her as he waited for her to respond, but she found herself speechless.

"I never knew you were so fond of me," Darkmoor continued with a grin.

"Not of you," Catherine muttered.

"The crow *is* me dear. And my vicarage, well... " Darkmoor trailed off.

"The crow is nice, and you're not him!" Catherine replied agitated.

"Catherine, Catherine, of course I am him. You've seen it with your own eyes, but I guess when I'm crow I'm not as powerful," and with that Darkmoor stood upright and released the perfectly cooked wolf-lizard from the skewer.

Not another word was spoken as Darkmoor cut open the beast and slapped the blood red meat into their bowls. Catherine wanted to object to eating with them, but a diet of bread and water had made her *very* hungry, so without waiting for Darkmoor to take his seat, she tucked into the fleshy, grizzly meat.

"So... " Darkmoor began with a mouth full of wolf-lizard, "what do you find so *fascinating* about me and the vicarage? I though everyone in Filius hated *us* both?"

Waiting until she'd swallowed her food, Catherine then looked up at him, "I guess, until now, I never had any reason to hate you. Since being a little girl I've always had the crow... *you* in my life and the vicarage. When I was naughty and sent to my room, I would sit on my window sill and stare across, wondering what it was like in there and who had lived there. I guess it sort of took me away from my life," Catherine's voice saddened as memories came flooding back. She looked away from him and quickly shoved another streak of meat into her mouth.

"Hmm," Darkmoor replied. "You wrote in your diary that you had to make sure I was ok, why? Why did you care?"

Catherine sat still for a moment, as Darkmoor's voice seemed to change. It wasn't raw or rough, it wasn't cold or callous and it wasn't steely or stern. It sounded broken.

Slowly Catherine looked up to meet his gaze, and there for the first time a small twinkle of softness sparkled in Darkmoor's eyes.

"Because…" Catherine started quietly then swallowing hard. Trying to contain her tears, she continued, "Because, y-o-u… " she started, stuttering over her words. She could feel her heart thumping rapidly.

"What?" Darkmoor asked impatiently, narrowing his eyes.

Catherine looked swiftly across at Logan and frowned. He was holding a leg of meat and like an animal himself was attacking it with his teeth. She shuddered at his disgusting eating habits then she looked back into Darkmoor's eyes, noticing a tiny splash of green circling the outside of his black.

"Go on," Darkmoor ordered.

"I was all alone, I had no friends to play with, no brothers or sisters to play with, and Mum and Dad were *always* busy with work, so I'd spend hours playing in my room, on my own. Then one day I heard you, well, Crow. It wasn't the normal caw but sounded like a cry, a lonely cry. I jumped up, looked out of my window, and there you... he was, sitting on the door step calling out. I sat and watched you flying around the vicarage for what felt like hours." Catherine stopped as Darkmoor broke away from her gaze and looked down at the table.

She studied the shadows which were cast across his narrow jaw line and up towards his perfectly formed cheekbones. His face appeared soft in the candlelight, and his eyes rapidly switched from side to side, searching for something to focus on. Then there, in the pit of her stomach, in the centre of her heart, taking over her whole body, was that pain of hurt and sympathy she had felt for him many times before. She couldn't explain it, she'd tried so desperately to block it out, but she knew that it was a part of her somehow. Growing up watching Crow had become a part of her and when faced with a chance to run and escape his evil castle, something deep inside of her had chosen not to.

Then like a dagger being thrust and twisted into her side, his soft, broken voice cut straight through her heart, "Why Catherine, why did you care, nobody cares about me, why did you?"

A small smile touched her lips, and quietly she asked, "Don't you remember?"

Without looking up at her, Darkmoor shook his head.

"You were my friend –"

"What?" Darkmoor interrupted.

"My friend, I know that might sound silly, but when I was four years old I really wanted a pet, but Dad, you see, he's allergic to them so every time I asked my parents they'd say no. I wasn't even allowed a goldfish. I just wanted to fit in because everyone at school had a pet, everyone except me. One day I was walking home from school with Mum and there you where, sitting on the doorstep, looking directly at me. You cawed so loudly you made my mum jump out of her skin. I remember chuckling to myself. Until then, I couldn't recall a time when someone had made me smile so much. The next day at school I kept smiling thinking of you, and I couldn't wait to see if you would be there again, and sure enough, you were! Every night I came home you would be sat on the step and every time you cawed. As I got older, I would sneak out, and I'd sit on the bench waiting for you. More often than not, you returned, and you'd just stare at me, just like we were friends. As time passed by I began to regard you as my own special pet, and like any eight-year-old who loves their pets, well that's how I felt about you. I wanted to keep you safe, and make sure no one took you away from me… "

As Catherine let her voice trail off, Logan burst into laughter causing bits of meat to spray out across the table, "Wait, let me get this right… " Logan spluttered. "You saw him as your *pet*?" another roar of laughter bellowed out of him.

"Silentium!" Darkmoor called across at Logan immediately causing Logan to compose himself.

Darkmoor rose to his feet, and like a lion hunting its prey he circled the table, "You love me like a child loves their *pet*?" Darkmoor quizzed. Still he didn't look at her, but Catherine shyly nodded.

"That's why you cared, because you thought I was *your* pet?" Darkmoor asked again, only this time his voice rose up.

"Yes and I know you won't admit it but I know you're not all bad. I know that crow is a *good* bird," Catherine quickly returned.

Darkmoor's voice was flooded with anger as he continued to march about the dining room, "I *am* the crow, I am *not* good –"

"But… but… " Catherine stuttered.

"No Catherine, no," Darkmoor stopped and finally looked down at her. She wrapped her arms around her body as she sensed his eyes upon her. Daringly she looked up at him, and she noticed that all traces of the soft green had departed from his eyes. The dark, cold, empty eyes were now fully black.

In a quiet yet chilling voice he stated, "I felt nothing for you. I played on your emotions. Don't you get it? I was waiting for Matthew and Jack to come and find me, that's all. You Catherine, you were the bait. We were *never* friends and we will never be… " then he lent across the table and whispered quietly to her, "… stop caring about me because when Matthew *does* return, I *will* kill you."

Her eyes prickled with tears, and this time she couldn't hold them back. One by one they rolled down her cheeks and splashed onto the table. Darkmoor turned his back on her, and he ordered Logan, "Take her back to the dungeon."

Logan instantly jumped up from his chair and rushed around the table. Grabbing hold of Catherine, he heaved her to her feet.

As Logan dragged Catherine towards the door, Darkmoor called, "Oh Catherine dear… "

Lifting up her heavy head, she spluttered, "Yes?"

"Sleep well," Darkmoor spoke wickedly with his most evil of grins.

"Come on," Logan said shoving her out of the dining room and out into the open theatre.

Once both Catherine and Logan had gone, Darkmoor looked into the fire. Shaking his head he chuckled out loud, "Catherine, Catherine, Catherine, how naive."

Thinking back over her words, something came to his mind. Something that was starting to annoy him almost like an impossible itch he couldn't scratch. Turning towards the door he headed out beyond the theatre and into his chambers.

"Damn girl," he cursed under his breath.

Grabbing the diary off the little table, he sat down on the edge of his bed. He held it out in front of him. His hands gripped so tightly around it that his fingers grew numb. Looking up from the faded pink cover, he darted his eyes in the direction of Dove. She sat like a statue in her cage with eyes firmly closed but she could hear his huffing.

"Hmm," he said towards her then releasing his grip, he opened the diary.

At first he flicked the pages open one by one not taking any notice of the words. Until something caught his attention:

September 2nd

I came home from school, and there he was again, waiting for me, probably making sure I was ok. My very own pet, I mean, who needs a dog or a cat or even a rabbit. I have my very own crow! I wonder if he sits there all day waiting for me to come home.

Then he turned to another page:

October 12th…

I've had a horrible day at school today. The girls are so mean, and they're always pulling my hair! Sometimes I feel so alone and Mum is too busy with work… wait I can hear him, calling for me…

Better go, Crow is calling. I'll write again soon xxx

Quickly flicking over another few pages, he noticed that time and time again how the name *Crow* appeared. Darkmoor was helplessly gripped by her words:

December 25th

It's Christmas day! I will take Crow his present later when Mum and Dad have fallen asleep. Going to go and open some more pressies!

Write soon xxxx

Darkmoor slowly pushed the covers of Catherine's secrets together. Placing the diary down at the side of him, he stood up and walked across to the window. There is was… Catherine's present.

She'd drawn a picture of a little girl resembling her and a crow stood at the side, both looking at each other. Somehow she'd made it look like the crow was smiling.

Darkmoor stared at it from a moment or two, then lifting his hand up, he stroked the picture with the back of his finger. Upon his touch he suddenly remembered back to the day Catherine had come skipping across the road to the vicarage. She had the picture rolled up under her arm to protect it from the snow. He recalled how she happily skipped down the path and placed her picture onto the doorstep.

Staring hard at the drawing, he felt an almighty pain beat inside his chest, piercing his heart.

"She's not scared of me?" he whispered. "She cares for me? No, no, no!" his thoughtful whisper soon turned into an angry shout.

"No!" he screamed. "No!"

Dove's eyes flicked open. She watched as the master of all fell down onto the cold hard floor. Shaking his head furiously from side to side, he muttered confusingly under his breath. Then in the blink of an eye, he was back to his feet, thumping his heavy boots onto the floor. He grabbed hold of the diary and furiously smacked his chamber door open. As the iron door crashed hard against the wall, it caused the room to rumble and with that, Dove's cage came crashing down.

"Catherine!" he called out around the castle. The wolf-lizards' were now present in the theatre. Upon hearing their master's distressed voice, they instantly stood to attention.

Without acknowledging them he walked past, his eyes were narrow and focussed. Grabbing a burning torch from one of the wall holders, he marched down into the dungeon.

Catherine was sitting with her back to him as her body turned cold with his presence.

"Catherine, look at me!" Darkmoor ordered firmly.

"No," she sternly replied.

"Catherine, I need you to look at me!" Darkmoor ordered again this time his voice was filled with venom.

"I don't want to look at you!" she shouted back.

"Fine, then I will do this without you watching!"

Holding out her diary in front of him, Darkmoor placed the burning torch beneath the pages. Aggressively the flames took hold of the pink cover.

Smelling the smouldering paper, Catherine quickly spun around.

"No," she said faintly, but then her voice suddenly awoke.

"No!" she roared towards him.

He didn't look at her, but he just carried on setting fire to her *precious* diary. Once it was completely ablaze, he flippantly tossed the diary down on to the floor and stamped down on it hard.

"There," he said looking down at the smoking book, "no more *happy* memories now."

"How could you? You know how much… I *hate* you."

Darkmoor stepped closer towards Catherine's cell. Pushing his head in between the bars, he looked directly into her eyes.

"Good," he whispered. "That is all I ever wanted. You see, Catherine, I'm not your pet. I'm not a nice little bird for you to play with. I am Darkmoor, the master of all, and you, my darling Catherine… well you really need to start realising that."

A deep buried anger bubbled up inside of her. His face was smug, as his eyes smiled gloatingly. She built up some phlegm in the back of her throat and projected it perfectly onto his cheek.

"Well, at last, your fiery side is coming out," he said pulling away from the bars and wiping off her spit, "I like it," he smirked wickedly.

Swiftly turning around, he headed for the stairwell. Without another word, he disappeared off towards the top of the castle, leaving her all alone.

Chapter Nine

The Final Meeting

Matthew was drumming his foot against the steel leg of the chair. His dad sat next to him with his arms folded. Every tap of Matthew's foot made Jack's body rumble.

"Matthew!" Jack shouted having had enough.

"What?" Matthew frowned looking up at his dad.

"Will you stop that *drumming*," Jack spoke through gritted teeth.

Matthew grinned and let out a deep sigh, "This is *such* a waste of time."

"This is your last appointment, after tonight that's it, just think of that," Jack remarked cheerfully.

Matthew smirked. He didn't want to be here, he'd never wanted to start seeing a doctor, but thankfully like his dad had said, this should be Matthew's last appointment.

Doctor Wicks' waiting room was colourful and bright yet slightly claustrophobic. Lime green striped wallpaper covered the walls, whilst an orange swirling carpet graced the floor. Positioned in the centre of the waiting room, directly in front of the receptionist's desk, was a row of blue cushioned seats. This was Matthew's tenth visit. Each time he'd only ever seen a handful of people waiting to be seen by either Doctor Wicks or Doctor Harrison.

The receptionist's desk curved round in an S shape and stood tall, hiding away Maggie Potts aka: *The Regimented Receptionist*. Getting an appointment here was like gold dust. First you had to overcome the obstacle that was Maggie and then and only then, if *she* thought you needed to see a doctor, would you get handed one of those golden tickets which read those *magical* words: *Congratulations you've been approved an appointment with your doctor…*

She'd never liked Matthew. She didn't like the fact that on most occasions he came out of his *special sessions* with another appointment already booked by the doctor. More often than not, Maggie Potts' face would screw up all red and puffy as if it was about to explode.

"How *dare* he give you an appointment without first consulting *me?*" Maggie had once muttered at Matthew.

Today she was observing Matthew from her watch tower. Occasionally she peeped over the top of the desk, glaring at him through her red rimmed glasses. Her bright red lipstick matched her red blusher. Her nose was petite and pointy. She wore her brunette hair up in a ponytail and her thick fringe rested on the tops of her eyebrows. When one of the doctors' doors opened, ready to welcome in another patient, the tapping of her pencil would stop and quickly she'd start typing on her computer.

"Mr Khan!" Doctor Wicks called across the reception area.

Matthew breathed heavy and looked up towards him.

"Matthew… shall we?" the doctor asked.

"See you in a bit, Dad," Matthew whispered.

"Yeah see you, Son," Jack half smiled as he watched his son heading off into the doctor's room.

Inside the doctor's office there was not a patch of lime green in sight. The walls were painted brilliant white and a huge window stretched across the back wall. As night had fallen, Doctor Wicks had drawn his blinds together, and only the light from the lamps dotted around lit up his tiny office.

Doctor Wicks closed the door gently behind him and just as Matthew had done a number of times before, he flung his coat on the stand and sat himself down in one of the brown leather armchairs. Opposite him was another armchair in which Doctor Wicks would sit, notes in one hand and a black biro in the other.

"Drink, Matthew?" Doctor Wicks asked.

"No thanks, I'm good," Matthew shook his head.

"So," he started whilst putting his cup of coffee down on the desk. Flicking open Matthew's file, he continued, "Hmm, so today is our last appointment."

"Yeah," Matthew muttered not looking up but finding himself focussing on the doctor's black suede shoes. Matthew heard the squeak of the leather chair opposite him, followed by a slurp of coffee.

"I need to ask you some questions before I sign you off… " the doctor started.

"Ok," Matthew replied slowly, trying to calm his racing heart.

"Matthew, are you going to look at me today?" Doctor Wicks asked drumming his pen onto the file.

At first Matthew wanted to shout, *no*! He thought about it and for a split second the word was on his lips, but then deciding that would only result in another meaningless bout of appointments, he reluctantly looked up.

Doctor Wicks was a plump man. His white buttoned shirt clung tightly to his belly, and he wore his pants far too high for comfort. His hair was thin on top and his two tiny eyes sunk deep into his head. The bottom half of his face was covered in short, stubbly hair. His moustache and beard grew into one, hiding his lips, and only when he spoke could you see a tiny, little mouth appear. His voice was smooth and sympathetic, and despite his unconventional looks, Matthew *did* like him, sort of.

"That's better," Doctor Wicks smiled. "Now, let's begin."

He looked down at his previously jotted notes, and after a few grunts and groans, he looked back at Matthew.

"Well dear boy, you've made great progress since our first meeting together. Can you remember what you told me when you first came to see me?"

Matthew slumped down into the chair. Of course he could remember… how could he ever forget?

"I'm telling you it is true, why won't you believe me?" I screamed at him.

"Matthew calm down," he softly spoke.

"Please," I pleaded, "you have to help me!"

"And I will, but first you have to calm down, ok?"

"He has her, the crow, Darkmoor, please, you have to understand!" I screamed again, trying to make myself heard, trying to make him understand.

"Why don't we sit down?" again he spoke softly whilst moving closer towards me.

"No!" I shouted. "No, we have to go back, Catherine –"

"Catherine Rose? Yes, I know she's missing, but please

if you just sit down we can talk all about it," he said nodding his head trying his hardest to make me listen. There was something about him, something almost trustworthy about him. He moved closer, placing his hand upon my shoulder, his softly spoken voice continued, "Matthew, I'm here to help you, I promise. Now please, come and sit down."

I looked deep into his eyes. His face was covered in stubbly hair yet somehow his smile shone through.

"Do you promise to help me?" I whispered.

"I promise," Doctor Wicks replied.

Matthew looked back at Doctor Wicks and nodded.

"Good," replied Doctor Wicks in a gentle, soothing tone.

"Since our first meeting and up to now, do you feel you've improved… moved on?" Doctor Wicks started tapping the tip of his black biro down onto file once more.

"I think so, yeah."

"Good, good and the crow you talked about… " Doctor Wicks glanced down to read Matthew's notes, "… the bird that changes into a man, Darkmoor, is how you referred to him, no more *big* adventures?" Doctor Wicks asked with a half smile present on his face.

Matthew forced a smile too. He thought for a moment before answering the doctor. Was now really the best time to bring up what had happened earlier at school? Or what Cassie had said about believing him that Darkmoor did indeed exist? Trying to stop himself from spitting out the whole truth and nothing but the truth, Matthew bit his tongue and shook his head from side to side, "No, no more adventures."

"Good, then I think we're all done!" Doctor Wicks triumphantly announced snapping shut Matthew's file.

"Really? That's it?" Matthew quizzed.

"Unless you have something else to share?" Doctor Wicks asked narrowing his eyes.

"No, no," Matthew quickly replied.

"Good, well, yes, that's it dear boy."

Doctor Wicks wiggled himself out of the armchair and offered his hand for Matthew to shake. A little awkwardly, Matthew limply placed his hand into Doctor Wicks' sweaty palm.

"Well, dear boy, I will miss our weekly session but I'm guessing you won't?" Doctor Wicks remarked jokingly.

"No, I guess not," Matthew agreed, pulling his hand out of the doctor's and quickly wiping off the extra sweat. "Thank you for helping."

"You're welcome Matthew, I'm glad I could. Now you're free to leave," Doctor Wicks said gesturing towards the door. "Although you never know, one day we may *meet again*!"

Matthew's eyes narrowed and stared vacantly at the doctor. Doctor Wicks had tilted his head back slightly. Laughing at his own words, Doctor Wicks' actions seemed to have been slowed down. Matthew's hands pounded with pain, slowly he blinked trying to awake himself, but this was real, he was awake…

I see the man of my nightmares. There he is, standing in front of me. His face narrow and gaunt, and his long sleek hair cascading freely down over his broad shoulders. Then with an air of arrogance he whispers those cold words, "So Matthew, we do meet again."

"Matthew? Matthew? Are you alright?" Doctor Wicks asked clicking his fingers a couple of times in front of Matthew's face.

Almost immediately Matthew remembered where he was and now, after finally being *signed* off, now was not the time to start thinking about Darkmoor.

"Sorry, yeah I'm fine. So Doctor, thank you for everything," Matthew smiled.

"Ok. Bye Matthew," Doctor Wicks said sounding slightly confused. He picked up his coffee, took a sip and nodded towards the door.

Matthew headed out of Doctor Wicks' room.

Jack was sat reading a car magazine when Matthew reappeared in the waiting room. Glancing up he saw his son happily walking towards him.

Jack flung the magazine on the empty chair next to him and looked down at his watch, "Finished already, wow that was quick?"

"Yeah, I'm not a nutter after all," Matthew replied sarcastically.

"Matthew," Jack sighed.

"Only joking Dad. Can we go now?"

Jack looked up and smirked, "Yeah come on, we've got to get to the village meeting."

"Please Dad, can I go home… " Matthew whined.

"No chance, you're grounded, remember… " Jack interrupted.

"But Dad," Matthew whined again.

"Son, you're coming with me and that's final."

Without another word Jack headed off through the double doors and into the car park.

Begrudgingly, Matthew trailed along behind.

- Chapter Ten -
Village Hall Antics

Matthew and Jack sat silently in the car as they drove through the snow covered village of Filius.

Street lights were all aglow as Jack entered the main street of the village, Chester Road. All the shops were closing up for another day. In the centre of the village was St. John's church. The top spire reached high up into the white sky and every Friday, without fail, the villagers would meet for bell ringing practice. From the centre, like a spider's web, weaved a number of streets, all of which were buried under glistening snow.

Chester Road stretched the full length of Filius until it eventually linked with the dual carriageway, which headed northwards up towards the larger towns.

At one end of Chester Road was Filius High, and situated at the other end was Filius Village Hall, unfortunately for Matthew, Jack was driving the car along Chester Road in the direction of the hall.

Each month some of the villagers gathered together to talk about different events they could organise, Church activities, fund raising events, actually it was a chance to meet up and have a gossip about the on goings of village life. Since Matthew and Jack had moved into the vicarage, they'd been continually talked about. All of the villagers believed the vicarage to be haunted and had stayed well clear for years.

Tonight however was a different sort of meeting altogether. Matthew swallowed hard as Jack drove onto the car park. He started to sweat and his breathing intensified.

"Matthew it'll be fine," Jack said reassuringly.

Matthew just smiled.

Jack parked the car in one of the few remaining spaces which was facing the village hall. The building was box shaped. A half glass, half wooden door welcomed you inside, and glass stained windows were dotted around the entire building box. Matthew sank down in his seat. He could hear the chitter chatter of the villagers already.

"Seriously, I don't think I can do this, Dad," Matthew frowned towards the village hall.

"Son, you'll be fine, trust me. Besides you're not the hot topic anymore. You know Mrs Mellor?"

"The old lady who lives next door to Cassie?"

"Yes, well rumour has it, that she… " Jack lowered his voice to a whisper, "… she has bunions."

"Dad!" Matthew smirked.

"Come on or else we'll be late," Jack said turning the car engine off and opening his door. "Come on, you'll be fine."

"Whatever you say, Dad," Matthew replied pushing open the car door.

At the front of the village hall you were faced with either walking up four steps or running up a ramp. Jack jogged up the steps and pulled open the door.

The volume of talking combined with the clatter of crockery crashing, produced one great loud noise.

Hesitantly Matthew stepped foot into the hall, and upon his cowardly arrival everyone fell silent.

"Come on, Son," Jack whispered from behind placing his arm around Matthew's shoulders.

Matthew forced a smile as the buzzing tones of whispering voices hummed around him. Every eye in the room eagerly watched his every step, and feeling a sudden urge to run, Jack tighten his grip around him.

"Son, you'll be fine," Jack whispered reassuringly. Then lifting his hand up, Jack waved over towards Pete and Julie. Together, Catherine's parents sat on the front row, left hand side.

Situated at the back of the hall were two tables, one containing three tall stainless steel coffee pots and a plate of biscuits, and the other one was containing five stainless steel teapots with another plate of biscuits.

Keeping charge of each table were Mr and Mrs Andrews. Both in their late 50's, grey hair, crumpled, wrinkly faces and clearly taking their jobs as coffee and tea makers very seriously.

Situated at the front of the hall was a stage on which a table was centrally located. A white table cloth was placed neatly over the top and a tumbler of water sat all alone upon it.

Taking up the hall were twenty plus rows of chairs. A number of people had taken to their seats already and others were quickly refilling their cups, whilst others were quickly dashing to the toilet.

"Drink, Matt?" Jack bellowed at Matthew in the mad commotion of the hall.

"I'll just have some juice," Matthew said passively.

On a round table top, away from the hot drinks, was a stack of plastic cups and a jug of orange squash. Matthew walked over towards it, and as he began to pull out the top cup, a familiar voice whispered from behind, "Can you get me one?"

Matthew frowned then turned around to look at Sophia, "Yeah."

"I thought you were grounded?" she asked abruptly, watching him take another cup and pouring her a drink.

"I was, still am, I think coming to this meeting is my punishment," Matthew muttered holding out two plastic cups.

"Ta," Sophia said taking one of the cups from Matthew.

Matthew smiled at her then taking a couple of sips of his juice, walked past her and down towards the front of the hall.

"Wait up Matt," Sophia called. Like a little lamb she started skipping quickly along behind him with her high heels clattering across the wooden floor.

"Great," Matthew whispered.

"We can sit together… if you'd like to, that is?" Sophia smiled at him, fluttering her long lashes.

Matthew simply nodded, and he followed her down one of the rows and sat down.

"So, you and Cass?" Sophia asked without warning.

Matthew looked shocked towards her, his eyes widened, "What?"

"Oh come on Matthew, not you as well?"

"I don't know what you mean… we're just –"

But before Matthew had chance to finish his sentence, Sophia had already done it for him, "- *just good friends*. Yeah right!"

For a few moments they sat quietly drinking their juice. Jack looked back a couple of times, just to check that his son was *still* here.

Jack was sitting on the front row next to Pete and Julie. Since Catherine's disappearance, Julie had lost a lot of weight, her frame was like a skeletons. Her hair hung un-brushed down over her shoulders and she constantly clenched a crumpled up tissue in her fist.

Matthew stared intensely at Julie and Pete. He'd told them over and over again where Catherine was but just like everyone else in Filius, they too thought he was crazy.

"I'm telling you the truth, Catherine is in Darkmoor!"

"Jack, get your son out of my house!" Pete shouted towards Dad, his face filled with anger as he held Julie in his arms.

"Come on Son," Jack walked across the room towards me. His arms stretched out wide as they motioned me to leave the Roses' house.

As if in slow motion I watched Julie. Her body shook uncontrollably, floods of tears poured down her face. Pete protectively placed his arm around his heart broken wife. I looked up and focussed on Catherine's school photo. It hung above the fire place in prime position. This was the picture everyone had seen, in the papers, on the telly and on leaflets. Catherine was sat smiling.

"I'm so sorry," I whispered, and then Dad's arms were wrapped around me, swiftly he pushed me out of their house. The sound of Julie sobbing was horrible.

Dad closed the door behind us and his eyes filled with rage, "That's it Matthew, I'm calling Doctor Wicks as soon as we're home!"

"Dad, please, no. I'm not making this up, I promise! Why? Why would I lie?"

"I don't know Matthew! But it stops right now!" Dad marched on ahead of me. I could still hear Julie crying and Pete repeated the same line over and over again, "Julie, she'll come home."

But I knew, I knew that was never going to happen…

"So if you don't fancy Cassie, who do you like?" Sophia spoke causing Matthew to jump. Slowly she moved closer towards him and once again fluttered her eye lashes.

"Soph, I think I'll go and sit with my dad." Matthew quickly jumped up and without looking back, he trotted down towards the front and sat himself down next to Jack.

"Phew… that was close," Matthew breathed out a sigh of relief.

Jack turned, "You ok?"

Matthew smiled, "Yeah, just had a lucky escape."

"Hi Matthew," Pete spoke.

"Hi Pete," Matthew replied. "Hi Julie."

Julie slowly looked up to meet Matthew gaze, vacantly she nodded towards him then turned to look away.

Matthew looked up at his dad who reached across and grabbed hold of Matthew's hand, "Don't worry, it'll be ok."

Pete stood up and turned to face the back of the hall, he waved to Mrs Andrews and silently mouthed to her that the meeting was about to start.

Pete chaired the meetings. Each month Pete would organise what was to be discussed in regards to the affairs of Filius and of course, the missing children. Tonight, in particular, was going to be all about the missing children. As Pete strolled up the steps to take centre stage, Matthew slumped down in his chair. He could once again feel everybody's eyes burning towards him. He was certain that it would only be a matter of time before everyone was once again accusing him of being a fantasy story teller.

Pete raised both of his hands and instantly silence fell.

"Right, well good evening everyone… " Pete started, "… thank you so much for coming out in this weather. As you all know tonight we are discussing –"

"What's *he* doing here?" a loud voice rumbled from the back of the hall.

Matthew's heart pounded, Jack quickly turned

around to see who the loud voice belonged to.

Stood at the back of the hall was an old man wearing a long black coat. His face was hidden underneath a hood. An arm stretched out, pointing directly at Matthew. Slowly but surely, the old man walked down the centre aisle, his coat moved from side to side and everyone started to whisper.

Matthew didn't dare look.

"Aren't you going to look at me, boy?" the old man asked.

Jack rose up from his seat and protectively shielded Matthew from him. "Who are you?" Jack demanded.

"Me?" the old man chuckled loosely. "I think the boy knows *exactly* who I am."

- Chapter Eleven -

Reuben's Mama

The old man stopped a couple of rows back from Matthew and Jack. Everybody in the hall was now staring silently at him, everybody except Matthew.

Jack bent down, "Do you know this man?"

Matthew couldn't find the words to say. His mouth and throat went dry, and as he stared deep into Jack's eyes, Matthew remembered back to the first time he'd heard that voice...

"You're Matthew Khan, aren't you?"

"Darkmoor... " Matthew faintly muttered.

Jack shook his head not wanting to believe the words his son was saying. Matthew slowly blinked before repeating the name, "Darkmoor, Dad, he's Darkmoor."

Jack swallowed hard. His heart thumped. He continued to look at Matthew then slowly he took his eyes off him, and there directly behind Matthew stood the old man.

"I think you should leave," Jack said trying to remain calm.

"Jack, everything alright?" Pete called over.

"Yeah, everything's fine, this *man* was just leaving!" Jack called back, not taking his eyes off the old man for a split second.

Slowly the old man lifted his hands up towards his face and started to lower his hood. His grey, matted hair fell scraggily around his narrow, gaunt face. His tired smoky grey eyes matched the complexion of his wrinkled and aging skin.

He leant over the top of Matthew and whispered, "If the boy asks me to leave then I'll go."

Matthew could feel his cold, icy breath on the back of his neck. He sat frozen to his chair, unable to move, unable to speak. Inside his head he wanted to scream out, "This is him… this is Darkmoor!" but he knew within a minute, Darkmoor would be gone, and once again everybody in Filius would make him the laughing stock.

"Matthew, Matthew, where has all your fighting spirit gone? Such a shame… " then the old man leaned in even closer and whispered chillingly into Matthew's ear, "… Catherine will be *so* disappointed."

"NO!" Matthew jumped to his feet and called out. Then, as he turned around to face the old man, everybody in the hall darted their eyes towards him and burst into a fit of laughter.

Jack suddenly jumped up from his chair and quickly pulled Matthew down into his seat, "What's the matter with you?"

"Dad that old man standing right behind me… " Matthew stuttered as Jack lifted his hand up towards him, shushing his son.

"Matt, there was no old man," Jack said confused by his son's reactions.

"But Dad, you spoke to him, he was right here, right behind me… " Matthew's voice trailed off.

"Son, that's enough!" Jack ordered him sternly, then looking up towards Pete, Jack called, "Sorry Pete, carry on!"

"We will talk about this later," Jack whispered down at Matthew.

"Dad I swear –"

But without saying another word, Jack threw Matthew a killer look, and slowly Matthew slumped down onto his chair.

"So, does everybody agree then, new posters of all the children who've gone missing? And I'll try the news reporters to see if they'll do another tea time showing."

The hum of deflation grew in the hall. Altogether six children had gone missing, all from Filius and

Matthew knew exactly where each one was. They could reprint flyers and posters, they could contact Sky news and post pictures in every newspaper in the world, but nothing, or no one could bring them back.

He sat quietly, listening to people chattering and muttering to one another. Pete tried to quieten them down but his efforts were in vain.

"Do you really think new posters, flyers, paper articles are going to make a shred of difference?" someone bellowed out from the crowd.

"I don't know," Pete said shrugging his shoulders. "But at least were doing *something*."

Another few voices started shouting out over each other, in a bid to get their point across. Pete was beginning to get flushed upon the stage, and he motioned his hands in an attempt to calm everybody down.

"I still think that vicarage has something to do with it!" an angry voice rose up over everybody else.

"Oh here we go," Jack whispered poking Matthew with his elbow.

"I don't think the vicarage has any part in the children going missing," Pete answered calmly.

"How do you know?" an elderly gentleman boomed then a chorus of voices joined in agreement, "yeah how do you know?"

"Because… " Pete started and when everybody had quietened down, he continued, "… because my Cathy didn't go missing anywhere near there."

A respectful silence fell within the hall. Nothing could be heard apart from the sobs of Julie. Pete looked over towards his wife, his face saddened and tears filled his eyes.

"Our precious daughter," he blubbered. He stepped away from the table and walked with his head bowed from the stage.

Jack stood up trying to sound positive, he patted Pete on the back, "She'll be home soon."

"Thanks, Jack," Pete looked down at Julie. "I hope so."

The hall was once again filled with a low buzzing noise of people speaking over one another and so the chattering and nattering continued.

Daringly, Matthew glanced behind him, sure enough, in full view was Sophia. She smiled and waved to him. At first he pretended he hadn't seen her, but when she waved again he felt obliged to wave back.

Taking this as an invitation to come and sit with him, Sophia jumped up from her chair and clip-clopped merrily towards him.

"Do you wanna get some fresh air?" Sophia asked him, her lips as good as touching Matthew's ear as she tried to be heard over the crowds of people.

"Eh?" Matthew sounded cupping his hand around his ear.

"I said… do you want to get some air?" she repeated, this time she said the words slowly, then tilted her head towards the back of the hall.

"Outside!" Sophia shouted pointing towards the exit.

Eventually Matthew realised what she'd been getting at and nodded. He quickly told Jack where he was going and followed Sophia through the uproar of the hall and out of the doors.

The cold night air upon his face.

"Thank goodness for that!" he remarked sitting down on the steps next to Sophia.

She brushed her long, sun-kissed hair to one side and looked into his eyes. "So… " Sophia started, "what was all that about in there?"

Matthew shrugged his shoulders, and breaking away from her stare Matthew looked up at the star filled sky.

"You wouldn't understand Soph, and believe me it is better that way."

"Maybe, but you could at least try me," Sophia replied trying to coax Matthew into revealing all.

"Believe me, you *really* don't want to know."

Sophia frowned and huffed. Wrapping her arms around her knees, she shuffled closer towards him.

Once again she fluttered her long lashes up at him, "I promise, it will be *our* secret."

"I don't think so," Matthew said shuffling away from her. But the further along the step he moved, the closer Sophia closed in.

"Look Sophia!" Matthew shouted jumping up. "You're a really nice girl and all, but no… me and you… no. I'm sorry."

"Seriously?" Sophia asked confused that Matthew wouldn't want to share his secrets with her.

"You really *do* prefer Cassie over me, don't you?" Sophia's face had started to glow red, pursing her lips she stood up.

"Cassie? Are you serious?" Sophia giggled loosely, waiting for an answer.

"No! No! I'm not into Cassie either, we're just friends, besides my head's all over the place and –"

"Well I guess it's true what Cameron says about you… " Sophia stood tall, as she folded her arms firmly across her chest and looked Matthew up and down. Then she whispered chillingly, "… you really are crazy… bird boy."

And with that, she stomped back up the steps, flung open the hall doors and slammed it to behind her.

Matthew slumped on the top step and stared upwards at the clear night sky, tiny stars flashed like

Christmas tree lights. He couldn't help but think of Catherine, all alone.

Completely lost in his thoughts, Matthew hadn't noticed an old lady appear at his side. Holding on tight to her walking stick, she managed another couple of steps towards him.

"Matthew Khan," she spoke. Her voice was weak and croaky, but that strong African accent was clear as day.

Matthew froze. He'd never heard that voice before, but he knew exactly who it belonged too.

"May I sit with you?" the lady quietly asked.

Matthew blinked a couple of times then slowly turned to look up at her.

She was just as Reuben had described, small and round and wobbled from side to side. Her big looped earrings swayed frantically about, and over the top of her lowered rectangular glasses were piercing dark brown eyes, which stared down at him. Her hair was cut short, like a boy's, with spiralling tight black curls.

Matthew gazed up at her in disbelief.

"Matthew, move over boy, my legs aren't has sturdy as they use to be," Josie told him.

Matthew was almost speechless, his emotions, having suddenly found himself in the company of Reuben's mum, had clearly affected him. He simply patted the step.

Josie grabbed hold of the railing, and slowly she lowered herself down onto the step. Placing her walking stick down at her side, she reached into the pocket of her thick, woolly, grey cardigan and pulled out a crisp, white hanky.

Matthew looked at her. She was real to him now, and he could finally put a face to the person he'd only heard about. Until now the link between Filius and Darkmoor was only possible through him, but now, sitting here was Reuben's mum, it made Darkmoor seem ever more real.

Seeing Matthew's eyes glazed over with water, she lifted up the hanky and passed it to him, "There you go dear."

For the past year Matthew had wrestled with his emotions. He'd pushed them deep down inside of him, determined not to let them show. But now, sitting here with Josie, knowing all too well of her sons' whereabouts and for the first time since leaving Camp Forgotten, Catherine and Darkmoor, Matthew sobbed.

She shuffled closer along the cold step, and placing her arm across his back, she slowly patted him, "Shush, shush, it's alright, you're gonna be just fine."

Together they sat. Matthew cried uncontrollably into the hanky, whilst Josie consoled him. The night air grew colder, and with the meeting inside the village hall still in absolute chaos, Josie whispered, "How about coming to my house for a steaming hot chocolate? I don't know about you boy, but my butt is getting cold on this step."

Through his sob's, Matthew laughed. Not giving a second thought to telling Jack, he nodded. Then tucking the used, snotty hanky into his jeans pocket, he stood up and offered out his hand for Josie to take. With one big heave, he hoisted her up off the cold step. She took hold of her trusted walking stick, "Come on young Matthew, we've got some talking to do."

Off he walked, side by side with Josie, heading in the direction of Reuben, Claude and Olli's home.

- Chapter Twelve -
A Painful Encounter

By the time they'd reached Orchard Road, the road that meets Acerbus Road, Matthew had stopped crying. Quietly he walked behind Josie. The street was dimly lit, and the echoes of cats fighting and wailing could be heard. Josie lead Matthew through a small wooden gate, up the path and onto the doorstep of her home. Glancing over his shoulder, he could see that standing all alone, with no lights on, was his home, the Old Victorian Vicarage.

Josie placed the key into the lock and turned it. Then placing her whole body against the door with all her might, she shoved it open. The smell of brewing coffee floated out and greeted them both.

Matthew eagerly followed her in. His body was shaking, partly due to the cold weather but mostly due to feeling nervous. What would he discover in here? What did she want to know? And what *did* she know?

Upon stepping through the doorway, a long hallway stretched out before him and was covered in a cream carpet. The stairs were situated on the right hand side of the hallway, and positioned against the left hand side was an old pine sideboard. Josie wobbled past it and headed down the hallway into the kitchen.

"Do you want some cream on your hot chocolate?" she called back.

"No thanks," Matthew replied politely.

Past the sideboard was a white varnished door. Matthew paused momentarily, wondering whether to enter through the door and into the front sitting room, or should he follow Josie into the kitchen. Turning around to face the stairs, he noticed a shoe rack. Positioned next to each other were three pairs of school shoes. Matthew knew exactly to whom these shoes belonged, and he smiled.

"I should box them up but I just can't bring myself to do it," Josie spoke up as she came back into the hallway, holding two cups of hot chocolate.

She took her eyes off the shoes, let out a deep sigh and moved past Matthew and pushed open the sitting room door.

"Come, sit down," she said pointing Matthew to the fabric beige armchair.

Matthew sat down and looked around the room. Situated on the back wall was a tall grandfather clock. Its tick-tock echoed about the room, chiming every half hour. Dozens of pictures hung around the walls, some of the boys and others of their father. Josie's rocking chair sat in the bay window looking out onto the street below. Next to her chair was the telly and towering next to that was a vase full of fake flowers, all purples, reds and oranges. A gas fire sat within a floral tiled surround and filled the room with warmth. Sitting on the mantelpiece were three silver framed pictures.

Matthew placed his hot chocolate down on the coffee table and smiled at the pictures. Reuben, Claude and Olli all stood proud in their school uniforms, smiling happily with their hands clasped. All three looked squeaky clean, and each one had tight, short curls. Matthew picked up the picture of Reuben and chuckled.

"What is it?" Josie asked.

"Let's just say he's changed *quite* a bit!" Matthew smiled before carefully replacing it on the mantelpiece.

"Why have you never been to see me?" Josie asked taking Matthew by surprise. Matthew lowered his head. Suddenly a sense of guilt came over him.

Slowly he raised his head to face her. She was now

sat in her rocking chair. The moonlight shone through the bay window and down upon her searching face. Somehow, she seemed so precious and fragile. Gripping both her hands around her hot drink, patiently Josie waited for an answer.

Matthew sat himself down in the armchair next to the fire. His heart beat fast, as his head was full of different excuses to give her. Nevertheless, he couldn't bring himself to lie to her.

"I'm sorry, I should have. I didn't want to upset you. When I told Pete and Julie about Catherine, they threw me out of their house. I guess, this is very selfish of me, but I'd gotten tired of people calling me a liar. I thought if I told you about your boys, you'd think of me in that way too."

There was a period of silence. Matthew reached out, picked up his drink and took some little sips.

Then Josie whispered those magical words, "I would have believed you. I do believe you Matthew… are they ok? My little Oliver, is he doing ok? My mister grumpy Claude? What about my big boy Reuben?" as she fired the questions at him, her voice broke down and tears flooded her eyes.

"They are doing just fine. Their hairs are a bit big and well, slightly on the wild side but other than that."

"I miss them so much. Every day is a living

nightmare, and I want to wake from it. What's it like? You know, D-a-r… "

"Darkmoor," Matthew filled in for her.

"Yes."

Matthew hesitated for a moment before finally finishing off his drink. He placed the empty cup on the coffee table and looked back towards the framed pictures, "He told me all about you, Reuben that is. He told me he loves you very much."

Josie smiled. She couldn't fight the tears as they streamed down her face.

"I'm sorry, I didn't mean to –"

"No, no it's fine… " Josie snuffled. "Please carry on."

"Well, Claude is still grumpy," Matthew smiled trying to lighten the mood.

"Yes, that's Claude," Josie smiled, pulling out another white, crisp tissue from her cardigan sleeve.

"Since their father passed away they became my whole life, they became my everything. Now I have nothing but emptiness," her face saddened once again.

"I was so worried about them, I'll never forget that horrible day. That nasty, evil man," Josie looked up sharply across at Matthew.

"Who?" Matthew asked confused, "which man? It was *Crow* who captured them."

"Crow?" Josie frowned, "what Crow?"

"The crow who lived in the vicarage before my dad and I moved in. He's behind all of this, I don't know how, but –"

"No! A crow, a silly bird? No he's nothing to do with it. It's him, all him!" Josie replied adamantly.

"But Reuben told me, he's convinced it was the crow. They were playing football in the street when Olli ran off after the crow and into the vicarage. Then he broke the globe."

Josie was more confused than ever. She shook her head from side to side causing her looped earrings to hit the side of her neck. Over the top of her glasses she stared at Matthew.

"I don't think you know the whole truth about your *new* home, do you?" Josie asked, her voice growing colder.

"Yeah," Matthew slowly replied, "my dad bought it off the internet."

"Really, just like that?" Josie asked clicking her fingers.

"Yeah… why? Who lived there, Josie?" Matthew asked sitting on the edge of the armchair, desperately wanting Josie to tell all.

"Just some lonely man, that's all," she said flippantly then turned to look out onto the street.

Matthew's eyes narrowed. He stared intently at her.

She rocked back and forth on her chair.

"Josie, please tell me what you know about the vicarage?"

Josie stopped rocking and glared across the room towards Matthew.

"I can't Matthew, I'm sorry, it's too painful for me."

"Please Josie, I need to know. If you tell me what you know about the vicarage then I'll tell you everything about Darkmoor, the truth, please just tell *me* the truth."

Josie looked away from him, "Ok," she finally whispered, "but I want to know everything."

Matthew criss-crossed his heart, "I promise."

- Chapter 13 -

Josie's Story

"Twinkle twinkle little star," I sing for the third time whilst rocking Oliver in my arms. Claude, my gorgeous little boy, is singing along with me as he builds building block towers on the rug in front of the fire.

"Mama, look, snowing," Claude says pointing excitedly out of the window.

Slowly I turn to look not wanting to awaken Oliver, "Why yes my sweetheart, indeed it is."

"No lady today," Claude tells me in a matter of fact way.

Turning back from the window, I look at him confused, "Lady, Sweetheart?"

"Lady with *big* belly," Claude asserts, thinking I should know exactly what he's on about.

I sit quietly for a moment, watching him build yet another tower, only to quickly knock it down and then start over again.

Not giving much thought to *who* the lady with the

big belly could be, I smile and continue to rock Oliver to sleep.

Suddenly, like a herd of elephants, Reuben comes crashing through the door on his scooter.

"Reuben! I've just got Oliver to sleep!"

I roll my eyes back and then give him my dragon look of disapproval.

Completely ignoring me, which at five-years-old Reuben was very good at doing, he then continues with his revving noises and heads straight for Claude and his tower.

"Be careful...Reuben watch Claude–" but my warning is too late as Reuben crashes into Claude, causing both him and his tower to go tumbling. Immediately I place Oliver down into his Moses basket, (who amazingly hasn't woken up with the noise) and rush over to help a crumpled up Claude.

"Reuben! What have I told you about racing around the house on your scooter?"

"But Mam," Reuben starts to whine. "It wasn't my fault... "

"I'm not interested in your excuses Reuben Freeman! Just go to your room and don't come down until your tea is ready!"

"But Mama... that's not fair!" Reuben starts but he is quickly silenced by my stern glare, and with a huff and a puff he finally turns around, lowers his head and stamps off upstairs.

"Silly boy," I say holding Claude in my arms. Heaving both myself and Claude up from the floor, I sit back down in my rocking chair by the window. Claude is all snuggled up on my knee, and slowly I push my foot on the floor and start the chair motioning back and forth.

The snow is falling softly outside. People buzz up and down the streets, determined that despite the wintery weather, they *will* get on with their daily business.

A few minutes pass, Claude and I sit in silence together watching the outside world from the warmth of our house. Just then, up from my knee, Claude springs, pressing his hands and face against the window, "Look Mama, there!" he calls excitedly.

"Who?" I ask looking past him and down the street.

"Lady with *big* belly," Claude replies.

And indeed, there she is. On the other side of the street, under a red poppy designed umbrella, is the lady with a large belly.

A white fleece coat is wrapped tightly around her body, making her olive skin glow beautifully. Her glossy black hair sways from side to side across her shoulders, and her feet are protected from the weather by her red wellington boots. Hanging loosely down against the front of her coat is a dark green scarf, which floats around in the winter's breeze. Her face is slim and radiant, her shoulders are small and slender and her big belly is in fact carrying a baby.

"Claude!" I chuckle. "She not fat, she's pregnant!"

Confused, Claude stares at me, "What?"

"Sweetheart, she has a little baby in her tummy."

"Baby?" Claude asks with a frown.

"Yes a baby, just like when Oliver was in my tummy, she too has a baby in her tummy."

Claude thinks about this for a moment, then a huge smile sweeps across his cheeky little face. Turning back towards the window, he simply remarks, "Oh."

"Hmm, I wonder where she's going?" I ask myself out loud.

"Mama, over there," Claude answers me pointing across the street to that big old house.

"What? The Vicarage? No she won't be going there."

Claude starts to nod his head, "Yep!"

"Are you sure?" I ask my detective two-year-old son.

"Yep," he replies with a certain nod.

"Hmm, that's odd. And what does she do in there?" I ask myself out loud.

Claude looks up at me puzzled, then shrugging his shoulders, he simply replies, "Dunno." And with that he turns, sit's himself back down in front of the fire and starts building his towers again.

I couldn't take my eyes off her. I have lived here all my life and never once had I seen anyone enter that old ruin. Well not anyone like her…

"Who was she?" Matthew asked.

"I don't know," Josie replied vacantly staring out of the window. "But when *he* disappeared, so did she," Josie continued turning back around to face Matthew.

Confused, Matthew shook his head, "Who?"

"A young man, handsome he was, but very strange, kept himself to himself. Wow, my word Matthew, look at the time!"

"Josie, who was he? What was his name?" Matthew asked rapidly.

"I've already told you far too much Matthew. You need to speak to your dad –"

"Josie please, his name, just tell me who it –"

"James!" Josie blurted out. "He was called James, that's all I know."

Just then Matthew's phone started to ring in his pocket. Shifting onto one side, Matthew reached down and pulled it out. The highlighted screen flashed:

Dad calling

"You'd better answer it, Matthew," Josie said softly.

Matthew smiled up at her and pressed the accept button. Before he had chance to speak, Jack ranted down the other end, "Where are you?"

"It's ok Dad, calm down… well if you stop yelling I will tell you where I am… yes Dad I remember, I'm grounded… ok, ok… I'm at Josie Freeman's house… what? No everything's ok… yeah, I'll be outside," Matthew ended the call, and awkwardly he smiled across at Josie, "I'd better go Josie, but thank you for the hot chocolate."

Within moments, Jack's car pulled up outside. His headlights filtered through the bay window and upon hearing the car door slam shut, Matthew jumped to his feet. Before he had chance to open the front door, Jack was hammering hard on the other side.

"Dad, Dad I'm here," Matthew said flinging open the door.

"Go and get in the car, Matthew!" Jack said sternly, his face full of anger.

"Dad I'm ok," Matthew said trying to reassure his dad.

In the hallway behind Matthew, Josie appeared.

"Jack," her African voice calmly spoke.

Looking past Matthew, Jack strongly asked, "What did I tell you about leaving my boy alone?"

"Dad it's ok, Mrs Freeman and I were just… "

"Car! Matthew! Now!" Jack ordered.

Without another word, Matthew scurried past Jack and jumped into the car.

"What have you told him?"

"Nothing," Josie replied.

"I don't believe you!" Jack boomed.

"Jack, the boy needs to know. He's not stupid!" Josie's voice rose up defensively.

"I *will* tell him, in my own time! He's *my* son Josie… "

"And if you're not careful Jack, you'll drive him away. How long do you think you can keep up this pretence? Tell him about James. Tell him about Anna, you owe him that," Josie's voice returned back to its normal calming tone. Stepping forward, she placed her hand upon Jack's shoulders.

Jack bowed his head. The raw emotions he'd buried years ago were now trying to bubble up but he wouldn't let them. Lifting his eyes to look at Josie, Jack whispered chillingly, "Stay away from *my* son."

Pushing Josie's hand away, Jack headed back towards the car, "You'll lose him Jack!" she called. "Just like Anna."

Jack stopped suddenly.

"If I tell him the truth, I'll lose him," Jack whispered sharply to Josie.

"And if you don't, Jack, you'll lose him," Josie softly whispered back.

"Then either way, I can't win." Turning away from her, Jack opened up the driver's door. He jumped in and started driving *his* son home.

Clever Crow sat perfectly still on the top of Josie's roof. Inside he was smiling, gloating, that at last his plan for revenge was starting to come together. Not only that but it was causing Jack and Matthew's relationship to fall apart. If nothing else, in all the *years* of his plotting and planning, then this one simple thing would be all the revenge he'd need.

Silently he unfolded his wings. The crisp clean night air gently touched his warm tingling body. Crow was untouchable and nothing was going to stop him.

Gracefully Crow followed them high above, as Jack and Matthew drove through the empty streets to their house. Crow perched himself on the chimney as they pulled up on the driveway. Matthew quickly jumped out and slammed the door shut. Crow had waited patiently for over a year to return, and he was certainly going to enjoy every single minute of his revenge filled plan.

Leaving behind his imprint in the frost, Crow hopped off the roof and cawed. Then off he flew into blackened night, ready and determined to position the last piece of his jigsaw in to place. All he needed to complete the puzzle was: one snow globe, one old man and a house full of people.

- Chapter Fourteen -

Clever Crow's Final Flight

"Catherine, please, you have to eat something," Logan begged Catherine as he held out a plate of stale bread and a glass of water.

Catherine shook her head.

"Catherine, please."

"I… said… no!" Catherine said sternly without giving him eye contact.

"Well, I'll leave it here for you then?" Logan asked shyly.

"Go away Logan, why don't you run back to your daddy?" Catherine teasingly asked.

"Catherine please don't do this, you know what he's like –"

"I know what *you're* like! You're a slimy little snake who is only after pleasing his father… well I'm not interested anymore, so go!" Catherine looked up at him, her eyes were washed free of colour, and that innocence which was once adorned on her face was no longer present, but instead anger, revenge and hatred now formed.

"If that's what you want," Logan spoke softly as he bent down to place the bread and water in front of Catherine's cell.

Clumsily, Logan dropped his set of keys. The clatter of the cold metal upon the hard floor made Catherine jump. Logan quickly looked up at her, "Before you ask, I can't."

"I'll eat the bread and drink the water. Please just one walk about, my legs need to learn to walk again, please Logan," Catherine begged.

Logan hesitated for a moment. Holding the keys to Catherine's cell in his hands, looking deep into Catherine's pleading puppy eyes.

"Ok, but only for a moment, he'll be back soon," Logan smiled anxiously at her. Slowly he positioned the key into the rusty padlock, and with a little force he managed to turn it. Hearing the click of the lock, Catherine stumbled to her feet. Dust floated off her, and once more clumps of her matted hair fell down on to the stone floor. Her cheeks started to slowly flush with colour as she half heartedly smiled at Logan. Carefully, and slowly, she shuffled her blistered feet towards him.

"Where are you?" an almighty voice thundered from the stairwell.

Logan's eyes flashed black upon hearing his father's voice. In panic he pushed Catherine back down onto the stone floor. Quickly he pulled the cell door too and clicked the lock closed.

"Logan!" Darkmoor called. "What are you doing, boy?"

"I… I… " Logan stuttered, "… nothing Father, I was just bringing her some bread and water, that's all."

Logan could hear Darkmoor's footsteps getting closer. Taking in a few deep breaths, Logan turned to face him.

Darkmoor looked over Logan's shoulder and glanced down at the lock, "Hmm, really?"

"Yes Father, look, see… she won't eat it though."

Darkmoor pushed Logan out of the way and glared at Catherine. She quickly tucked her head into her knees, determined not to look up at him.

"Catherine," Darkmoor called in a sweet yet arrogant voice.

"I've brought you something," he continued reaching down into his coat before revealing a new pink bound book.

Catherine slowly lifted her head. Taking in a few sharp breaths, she stumbled once again to her feet. Nervously she moved towards him as he stepped closer to the bars of the cell. Looking deeply into his eyes, she hoped for the hundredth time, to find something of Crow in them.

A tiny smile appeared in the corner of his mouth, and just like she'd seen at dinner, a splash of green appeared.

"I'm sorry I got so angry with you. I should never have burnt your diary. My plan, you see Catherine, my plan is starting to come together, and I want, I need you on *my* side," Darkmoor spoke softly.

"What?" Catherine asked somewhat surprised.

"My plan, revenge on Matthew, Jack –"

"Mr McKendry? What's he ever done to you? And Matthew, he's just a boy," Catherine interrupted, trying to make sense of Darkmoor's words.

Darkmoor didn't reply, but instead he looked into Catherine's searching eyes. Then there it was again, that pull of pain he felt whenever he was near her, like an almighty thump of guilt. He reached a hand carefully between the bars, but as he moved his hand towards her, she simply pulled away.

"Don't touch me," she muttered.

Her words felt like a dagger in his side but doing what Catherine wished, he slowly pulled his hand back.

"Hmm… I thought this," Darkmoor said lifting up the diary in front of her, "this would maybe make us friends again."

"Friends?" Catherine quizzed. "We've never been friend, and besides why would I want to be *your* friend?"

Darkmoor fell silent. He looked at her, completely stripped of her innocence, the innocence that he'd viciously taken away from her.

"Father, I'm on your side," Logan piped up from over Darkmoor's shoulder.

Upon hearing his voice, Darkmoor quickly snapped his neck around to face Logan. His eyes had changed back to the colour of the night and his soft smile was replaced by a sinister smirk.

Darkmoor took a couple of steps towards his son and patted his shoulder. Logan's smile almost mirrored that of his father's, and without looking back at Catherine, Darkmoor dropped the new diary on the floor. Together, Darkmoor and Logan made their way up the stairwell.

Catherine's eyes filled with tears, and like a crumbling building she collapsed down onto the floor. The bread and water were within her reach. Shuffling and stretching herself, she just about managed to retrieve them.

Upon finishing her *mini feast*, her eyes fell towards the new shiny diary. It laid there shining gloriously like a star next to her old black burnt one.

"On *his* side," she muttered to herself as she switched her eyes from one diary to the other.

"Why!" she shouted.

She couldn't help but think of Matthew and Jack, and what did he want with them? Why would Darkmoor want revenge? And what did he want revenge for?

The more she questioned his actions, the more she could feel her fighting spirit returning. Suddenly, like at bolting of lightning, it came to her, "Dove!"

"Ok! Ok! I'm on your side! Darkmoor!" Catherine shouted out, knowing that he *would* hear her.

Almost immediately there he was, in front of her cell. A huge smile swept across his face and reaching down into his coat, he pulled out the golden key.

"What made you change your mind?" Darkmoor asked inquisitively, flipping the key across his knuckles.

"I don't want to be in here anymore, so if being on your side means that I can leave this dump, then I guess I'm with you," she said confidently.

"Good! But don't try anything silly, Catherine. I *will* kill you!" he said chillingly, narrowing his eyes.

Swallowing hard, Catherine simply nodded.

Not taking his eyes off her, he placed the key into the lock. Catherine scrambled to her feet and stepped towards him. He turned the key and the click made her heart jump. Darkmoor pulled the padlock off the cell and accompanied with the golden key, placed them deep into his coat. Then for the first time ever, he offered out his hand for Catherine to take.

Catherine stopped. His kindness unnerved her, but then almost immediately, Darkmoor snapped his hand away and stood tall before her.

"Come on, we need to get you fed!" he called walking away.

Sheepishly she followed behind him. Every step was an effort to take as her bones creaked together. Desperately trying to block out the pain, she set foot onto the first step which lead up to the theatre.

Lined up in the theatre were several wolf-lizards. Like statues they stood tall, mighty and powerful, and in front of them stood Logan. Upon seeing Catherine a soft smile appeared on Logan's face, however, feeling his father's eyes upon him instantly wiped clear his smile and he stood to attention.

"We're getting ready for battle, Catherine!" Darkmoor called, relishing the prospect. "My beautiful monsters are ready, those meaningless campers are getting ready to face me, just one last thing to put in place then the *party* can begin," Darkmoor threw his head up towards the sky and laughed.

Catherine gazed over towards Logan, who hadn't moved an inch, and she couldn't help but feel pitiful for him.

"Boy!" Darkmoor called towards Logan, "come here."

Lowering his voice, Darkmoor whispered something to his son, and just like a puppy dog Logan trotted off out of the theatre in the direction of Darkmoor's chamber.

Catherine wrapped her frail arms around herself. Darkmoor smiled over towards her, but his face was full of evil and darkness, just as she'd seen many times during the past year.

Logan rapidly came trotting back into the theatre, cupping something in the palms of his hands. He smirked smugly, as Catherine noticed that his eyes were pure black.

Unable to see what Logan had been to retrieve, she tiptoed closer towards them both. Upon hearing her movements, Darkmoor turned abruptly, "Come here Catherine, you can see what we have."

Hesitant at first, Catherine stayed still, but then as Darkmoor turned his back on her, she became more intrigued and walked over to his side.

There it was: the link from Darkmoor to Filius. Sitting majestically in the palm of Darkmoor's hands was the snow globe. Catherine gasped loudly, making Darkmoor grin. Gently Darkmoor stroked his thumb over the glass.

"Logan, make sure Catherine doesn't do anything stupid whilst I'm gone."

"I promise, Father," Logan replied vacantly, obviously transfixed by the glass globe.

"Gone?" Catherine quizzed, "gone where?"

Darkmoor laughed loosely, "To deliver this back to Matthew."

Catherine's jaw dropped. Her heart raced at the mere mention of his name.

"But you," Catherine started.

"Now, now Catherine, you said you were on *my* side," Darkmoor quickly reminded her.

"Yeah, I am… " Catherine stuttered, trying to sound convincing.

"I am… I promise I'll behave," Catherine added, looking first at the globe then back to Darkmoor.

"Good!" Darkmoor replied.

Handing back the globe to Logan, Darkmoor stepped closer to his wolf-lizards.

"Soon my beautiful creatures, soon revenge will be ours and we will have an almighty feast beyond our wildest dreams!"

The wolf-lizards howled joyfully at their master's promise, then lifting his hands up into the sky, Darkmoor clapped twice, and instantly the wolf-lizards retreated one by one out of the theatre and down the alley way.

Catherine looked across at Logan, whose black, steely eyes were firmly fixed upon his father.

"Stand back Catherine!" Darkmoor called, motioning her to step back against the theatre wall. Logan had already positioned himself there, carefully gripping on to the precious snow globe.

Once all the wolf-lizards had disappeared from the castle, thick living fog formed and made its way up through the alley which covered the theatre floor. Darkmoor opened his arms wide to greet it. Like a whirlwind the fog spun itself around Darkmoor's tall, slender stature, soon his body was completely covered in the white fog.

Catherine closed her eyes tight.

Up from the ground Darkmoor rose, now completely cocooned in the fog. He could feel his fingers closing together, his arms cracking in two, feathers started pushing themselves up his throat and out of his mouth. His face pulled tight, and his eyes started to shrink. His body was transforming, like it had done time and time again, but this time he hoped it would be his last, and then he would be free. The pain of his bones breaking, his muscles twisting, and his face being pulled and torn, would hopefully be worth it after today.

Catherine couldn't bring herself to watch however Logan looked on in awe. He was completely mesmerised by his master's transformation.

The theatre fell silent and cold. The icy fog started

to slither away, pleased with its performing miracle. Sensing the fog's departure, Catherine slowly dared to open her eyes.

Replacing Darkmoor was Clever Crow.

She couldn't help but smile. An overwhelming warmth instantly filled up inside of her and although she knew his true identity, to her, Crow *was* different.

"Hello you," she whispered bending down to stroke his coat. Happily Crow hopped towards her, welcoming her warming touch. Logan's eyes widened in amazement, "You *do* know that's my father, right?" Logan asked amused.

"Yeah, of course, it's just, well he's... *different*," she smiled up at him.

"Yeah, that's because he is *different*, he's a bird," Logan smirked.

Rolling her eyes back, she looked back down at Crow. Finally she took her hand away and stood back. Logan stepped forward and very gently tied the snow globe around Crow's feet.

"There Father, you're all set. Be careful, it'll be quite heavy," Logan said caringly.

Crow looked up at Logan and cawed in annoyance. He'd carried the snow globe before and never once had had any problems. Then he looked up at Catherine.

She smiled down at him, and as he unfolded his

wings from beneath his sleek black coat, Catherine quickly stepped in front of him, "You don't have to do this, please. I know you're better than this."

Crow stared at her, his wings hung still.

"Please," Catherine whispered breathlessly, her eyes prickling with tears.

"Caw! Caw!" Crow called out and up he hopped into the sky above. The snow globe dangled freely behind him, and within seconds he soared up and out of the castle. Crow and the globe disappeared.

Hoping that this would finally be his final flight, Crow flew with all his might. The stillness of the night helped him on his journey. Lying like snow across the whole of Darkmoor was a blanket of fog, which glistened like crystals in the moonlight. And as the River of Souls came into view, Crow swooped down.

Dutifully, his beautiful angels dived out of the misty lagoon to greet their master, and like elegant mermaids they dived in and out. The river swirled as tiny ripples of fog lapped onto the river bank.

Crow focused his stare upon the woods beyond the river, the woods in which Camp Forgotten was buried. Soon the camper's who were living deep within, would realise who Clever Crow really was and unbeknown to them, their *precious* mud huts would be burnt to ashes.

With a sense of triumph and sweet revenge, he

darted over the river and up high above the woods. Upon hearing the sounds of the camp, Crow slowed himself down and hovered above the towering fires flames. He couldn't quite make out their chatter but just to let them be aware of his presence, Crow cawed down. His tiny beady eyes smiled intently with glee as the rushing and panic echoed up towards him.

Quickly tilting his head backwards, he glared into the blackened depths of the sky. An overwhelming hatred, which he had lived with for years, filled his eyes.

Despite the pull of the snow globe, Crow remained focussed. Wrapping his wings around his body, like he'd done hundreds of times before, Crow shot through the night like an arrow, an arrow set for the kill.

Chapter 15

Matthew's Birthday Misery

"Dad I told you, I don't want any fuss," Matthew whined as he followed his dad around the vicarage.

"Son, it's your birthday, and besides after the year we've had I think you deserve to let your hair down," Jack smiled, ruffling Matthew's hair.

Jack was trying to make things right with Matthew after the whole Josie incident. He'd banned Matthew from going anywhere near her house but knowing that Josie knew more than she'd been letting on, Matthew had been tempted to find out more. However, begrudgingly he obeyed his dad's wishes and now as a reward, Jack was throwing him a birthday party.

Cassie had helped out too, although her idea of help was putting up a poster on the school's notice board and inviting everyone from school, which naturally included Sophia *and* Cameron!

Not only had the party been the talk of the whole school, it was also the talk of the whole village, much to

Matthew's annoyance. He'd started to think he was the only person who *didn't* want to attend but given the fact it was to take place at the old vicarage, he really didn't have much of a choice.

His dad and Cassie had gone full steam ahead, and the party was due to start in half an hour. Jack had put balloons up in both the sitting room and the dining room. The spiral staircase was covered from top to toe in coloured streamers with each step alight with candles. The kitchen had been taken over by a mountain of food which was covered by cling film. A stack of plastic cups and paper plates towered high on the breakfast bar and next to them were various types of bottled drinks. And now Jack was busily going from room to room putting out party poppers.

"Dad really, I'm not four," Matthew said following Jack around, picking up the poppers as quickly as his dad put them down.

"Matthew, look, your guests will be arriving soon. You go and get changed, and I'll finish putting the food out," Jack said cheerfully walking past Matthew.

"But Dad, I am changed!" Matthew said looking at himself.

"Oh ok, well, just go and change into your *smart* jeans, I've ironed them and put them on your bed."

"Ok," Matthew sighed. As he turned to walk up the

stairs, the first knock at the door came.

"Matt, you'll have to get that, the jelly's just spilt!" Jack called from the kitchen.

Matthew rolled his eyes. As if it wasn't bad enough that most of the school would be coming but to be having jelly at his party, Matthew was *not* impressed.

Dragging his feet along the hallway, Matthew slowly opened the door. Standing on the doorstep were Cassie, Sophia and Amber, all with huge grins across their faces and eyes filled with excitement.

"Hi," Matthew mumbled.

"Hi!" Sophia and Amber called over excitedly in unison, "can we come in?"

"Yeah, yeah of course," Matthew replied opening the door up fully, trying to sound more enthusiastic.

Amber and Sophia quickly trotted past him and headed directly for the sitting room. Within seconds, out of the stereo blasted Katy Perry.

"Katy Perry? Really?" Cassie asked Matthew.

"It's my dad's," Matthew replied sarcastically.

"I tried to make them wait until eight, but you know what they're like. Anyway, happy birthday," Cassie smiled, then lifting up her present continued, "this is for you. I hope you like it?"

Matthew reached out and took hold of it. It was a

small rectangular box, covered in football wrapping paper. The tag attached read: *Happy Birthday Matthew xx*

"Do you want me to open it now or –"

"No wait until afterwards. It's nothing much –"

"Oh, ok well thanks," Matthew whispered as he leaned in to kiss Cassie on the cheek.

Instantly, her pale snow white complexion flushed red.

"Er, you two, are you joining the party or what?" Sophia called over which made both Cassie and Matthew giggle embarrassingly.

"Yeah we're coming!" Cassie called back from the doorstep, then stepping past Matthew, headed into the sitting room.

Matthew was just about to turn and follow Cassie into the vicarage, when regretfully he heard Cameron Thomas' grunting voice echoing from down the street.

For a moment Matthew thought about closing the door and locking it. But unfortunately it was too late, as Cameron's round chunky body came into view at the end of the driveway. Followed, as ever, by his *young* tribe of followers, who at 7.30pm should *really* have been at home, but nevertheless, here they *all* were.

"What's up Matt," Cameron called across the garden as he trudged down the path.

"What do you want?" Matthew quizzed.

Cameron smirked, then looking down at his tribe he started to laugh.

"We were invited to a party!" Cameron said sarcastically, whilst wriggling his hips side to side.

"Cassie," Matthew muttered under his breath.

"So… " Cameron started, "… can we come in and boogie?"

Cameron was wearing baggy jeans which, just like his school pants, hung way too low. His matching denim jacket was unzipped revealing his Homer Simpson t- shirt which aptly read: *"Doh!"*

Matthew looked at him suspiciously wondering what Cameron was up to.

"Well?" Cameron asked again, as he stepped closer towards Matthew.

"Hi boys come on in, I'm Jack," Jack spoke up, brushing past Matthew.

"Oh you must be Mr Khan then?" Cameron's voice changed from the grunting gruffalo to that of an angelic choir boy.

"I'm Mr McKendry, but please call me Jack," Jack replied happily welcoming Cameron and his tribe into the vicarage.

Cameron patted Jack's upper arm, "Right you are, Jack!"

Jack, Cameron and his groupies walked off into the

vicarage, leaving Matthew alone on the doorstep.

At first he looked up into the starry night sky, and then his eyes fell across the road at number 23. The downstairs curtains were pulled together, blocking out the outside world. Above the front room was Catherine's bedroom: dark, empty and lifeless. Her curtains had remained opened, and as Matthew stared at her window, he tried to imagine Catherine standing there waving down at him. But her face had started to fade from his memory, and all he felt was guilt.

Slowly he turned around and stepped back into the vicarage. He shut the door behind him and was welcomed by the chorus of chattering, laughter and booming music.

More and more guests arrived, each one welcomed in freely by Jack and as the night continued, so did the fun.

Hiding himself within the bushes, in his familiar place, was Crow. He was waiting for the perfect moment to present Matthew with his *special* birthday present.

He listened to the singing, screaming, cheering, and his body felt every thud of the bass as it vibrated along the ground. The more he waited, the more he grew sick of the sound of enjoyment. There was only one time he could remember when the vicarage had been the focus of a party and that was the worst night of his life. Now it was Crow's turn to make this the worst night of Matthew and Jack's life.

Twisting his beak around, Crow managed to cut through the string, releasing the globe. It rolled several times along the ground until eventually it came to a standstill on the driveway. Crow cawed in annoyance with himself, and quickly hopping out from underneath the bushes, he used his beak to roll the globe back under the hedgerow.

Matthew was in the kitchen. His head pounded as if a drummer was in there beating hard away. He poured himself a glass of juice unaware that his dad had been calling for him.

Suddenly the kitchen door flung open, "Matt, your dad wants you!" Cassie shouted trying to make herself heard over… *'Mama do the hump'*.

"What?" Matthew mouthed back.

"D-A-D," Cassie mouthed back pointing down the hallway.

"Oh!" Matthew said placing his drink down on the worktop.

The hallway was crammed full of people, half of whom Matthew didn't even recognise from school, but Cassie had reassured him that everyone here was from Filius High, just maybe not *his* year.

Stretching up onto his tiptoes, Matthew managed to

look over the heads in the hallway and saw his dad standing at the front door.

Then, as if in slow motion, Matthew glanced towards the doorstep. His heart pounded, the music seemed to fade, and there he stood: *the old man from the car boot sale.*

He looked up towards Matthew. A long black coat covered his frail body. His hood partially hid his face, casting a dark shadow across it. His grey aging eyes pierced through Matthew like a dagger.

Within his hands he was gripping a shoebox, and without hesitation Jack happily accepted it from him. Once he'd placed it into Jack's hands, the old man wickedly grinned in Matthew's direction. Suddenly, in one clear movement, his grey eyes flashed black. The old man turned around and stepped off the doorstep, and off he disappeared back into the dark canvas of the night.

"No!" Matthew cried painfully as he started to push his way through the crowd.

"Matthew, what is it?" Cassie panicked.

"It's him! Move!" Matthew shouted over the music.

"Dad! Dad!" Matthew called, "don't open that parcel whatever you do!"

"Matthew, *you're* scaring me," Jack frowned as his son came charging through the crowded hallway.

Matthew looked straight into Jack's eyes, "Dad,

please just stay there. Please, promise me Dad –"

"Ok, ok, calm down Matt. What is it?" Jack asked but tentatively Matthew carried on out of the vicarage in pursuit of the old man.

The old man was walking swiftly down the driveway, his coat swaying from side to side. When he reached the bottom of the driveway, he let out an evil laughter which filled the night sky.

"Wait! Stay there!" Matthew called after him but the old man continued.

Sprinting down the path, Matthew grabbed the back of his coat and forcefully flung the old man around to face him, but immediately upon Matthew's touch, the coat emptied of life and the old man's shell-of-a-body had vanished. Both anger and hatred filtered through Matthew as he squeezed the coat tightly between his fingers.

"No!" Matthew cried up to the sky. "No!"

Suddenly, from the side of the driveway, rustling and crunching sounds floated on the icy breeze. Matthew stood frozen as the muffled noise became tiny footsteps.

Matthew slowly turned, then letting out a heavy breath, he muttered, "We do meet again."

Crow bowed his head towards the floor. All the while his beady eyes remained focused upon Matthew's face. Both joy and excitement were bursting through

Crow's entire body, nevertheless trying to contain his emotions, he stood still.

"Where is Catherine? What have you done with her?" Matthew asked, his voice rising up in anger. Crow just stared coldly at him.

"Wait… the shoebox… " Matthew looked back at the vicarage. The party was still in full swing, and suddenly realising what had just been delivered, Matthew threw the coat onto the ground and ran frantically up the driveway towards the vicarage.

Crow cawed out joyfully then he opened his majestic wings and hopped up into the sky, and off he headed back into Darkmoor, ready and waiting for Matthew's return.

- Chapter 16 -

The Truth Will Out

"Everyone out!" Matthew shouted as he ran back into the vicarage, "I said everyone out!"

"Son," Jack spoke still holding the shoebox in his hands. "Son, what is it?"

Matthew turned to his dad, his face full of panic, "Dad, we need to get everyone out, now!"

"But –"

"He's back Dad, Crow is here."

Jack's face dropped. His eyes saddened as he watched his son fearfully race around the house forcing everyone to leave. Cassie cut the music, and like a herd of elephants, the children ran out of the vicarage.

Jack stood shocked, and the palms of his hands began to sweat.

"Matthew, stop this, you're scaring me," Cassie screamed as Matthew tried to push her out of the door. Stubbornly, Cassie continued, "No Matthew! I'm not going until you explain what's going on!"

She stood in the doorway with her arms folded, alongside her stood Amber and Sophia, all waiting for some sort of explanation.

"Cassie, please, just trust me, you have to go," Matthew pleaded but Cassie was having none of it.

"It's Crow, he's here, he's back," Matthew whispered sharply.

Jack stepped towards his son, "Matthew you have to stop behaving like this… "

"But Dad –"

"Nice loo for a number two. Hey, where did everyone go?" Cameron called from the top of the staircase.

"Everyone's left Cam, Matthew's going crazy," Sophia piped up, twirling her finger at the side of her head.

"Bird boy," Cameron grinned, "can't you just be sane for *one* night?"

Matthew could feel his temper raging up inside of him, as he stepped closer towards Cameron, who casually jumped off the bottom step and walked confidently towards him.

"Fancy a go then, Matthew?" Cameron coaxed.

"Boys!" Jack shouted, "I don't think so… wow, this parcel seems to be getting hot."

"Dad," Matthew calmly spoke, "put it down, carefully."

"I don't think I can… " Jack looked up at Matthew confused. His eyes filled with anxiety as they flicked from Matthew then back towards the box. Desperately, Jack tried to place the box down onto the sideboard, but his efforts were useless as the shoebox was now firmly stuck in the palms of his hands like glue.

Matthew looked up at the girls then back over towards Cameron, "You all need to leave."

"No way!" Sophia said assertively, "we want some answers!"

"Yeah, bird boy," Cameron happily piped up, flapping his arms mockingly.

"Look, you have to go, it's for your own good," Matthew begged.

"Is it me or is that box glowing?" Amber asked vacantly, pointing over towards the shoebox.

"Woah!" Cameron called out in amazement.

Sophia and Cassie gasped. The shoebox was glowing bright yellow and the snow globe, hidden inside the shoebox, was beginning to come to life.

Jack's face screwed up as the heat intensified. Trying to help his dad, Matthew pulled the lid off the box and placed both hands inside. Matthew slowly pulled out the burning glass globe.

The empty box fell out of Jack's hands. Matthew cupped the globe, and instantly the light shone brighter.

Soon the light was so bright that everyone was forced to close their eyes as it is glowed like the sun throughout the vicarage. Matthew's hands felt like they were on fire, but he knew that at any moment the globe would crack.

And sure enough, an almighty light flashed, the globe smashed, and within an instant, the light vanished and so too did the vicarage.

Matthew, Jack, Cameron, Cassie, Sophia and Amber, all found themselves lying face down on the muddy bank of the River of Souls. The atmosphere was as cold as ice, the smell of rotten fish and sweat filled up the dark, gloomy sky which was now surrounding them.

On the other side of the river stood Darkmoor, Catherine, Logan and his army of wolf-lizards. A roaring howl of approval cut through the air at the sight of Matthew.

Catherine vacantly stepped forward and whispered breathlessly, "Matthew," but Darkmoor swiftly grabbed her arm, and he pulled her back.

Chillingly, he darted his eyes at her, "Remember whose side you're on, Catherine."

"Matthew! Matthew! Welcome back!" Darkmoor called tauntingly across the river.

Darkmoor's voice sent shivers down Matthew's spine. One whole year he'd been fearing this moment, knowing all too well he would somehow return.

Pushing the palms of his hands firmly down into the mud, Matthew gradually lifted himself up. On one side of him were Cassie, Amber and Sophia, and on the other were Cameron and his dad.

"Where are we?" Cassie asked as she started shaking.

"What did you do, bird boy?" Cameron called over brushing the mud from his baggy jeans.

"Oh no!" Sophia screamed in shock. "Look at my shoes!"

"Darkmoor, we're in Darkmoor," Matthew answered faintly.

Nervously, they all looked across the white misty river to where Darkmoor and his monstrous army stood.

Darkmoor's wicked grin stretched across his face as he *arrogantly* waved towards them. Amber *naively* waved back.

"I see you've brought your friends with you!" Darkmoor shouted over, which was accompanied by hungry howls from the wolf-lizards. "My beautiful creatures are *very* thankful!"

Daringly, Matthew looked across the river to meet Darkmoor's gaze. But instantly his eyes darted towards the tiny wreck of a skeleton girl who stood beside him.

"Catherine," Matthew gasped as if the wind had been knocked out of him.

Feeling vulnerable, Catherine wrapped her arms

tightly around herself, and quickly she tucked herself in behind Darkmoor.

"Hurts, doesn't it?" Darkmoor muttered to her. "Seeing someone you love with someone else."

Catherine shrugged her shoulders, "I don't love him," she replied looking down at the floor.

"No of course not, because you're *only* a girl and far too young to be in love. Is that what they tell you?" Darkmoor questioned, but Catherine didn't respond.

Looking back across the river, Darkmoor called again, "Matthew!"

"Stand behind me, don't look at him," Matthew instructed everyone and without being told again, Cameron, Cassie, Amber and Sophia all hid behind him.

Tears ran uncontrollably down Amber's face, and comfortingly Sophia placed her arms around her.

"Fancy a hug, Cass?" Cameron asked opening up his arms in the hope of Cassie rushing into them.

"No Cam, I'm good, thanks," Cassie smiled falsely. Instead she stood next to Matthew, and slowly she tried to place a hand into his but something in him had changed after seeing Catherine. Rather than accepting her hand, he coldly pulled his hand away.

Jack stood facing his son. He placed both of his hands upon Matthew's shoulders.

"Oh look at that, Father and Son bonding!"

Darkmoor shouted joyfully, but then his voice turned rough and raw.

"Jack McKendry!" Darkmoor roared.

A look of confusion spread across Matthew's face, and slowly he moved away from Jack, "How does he know that?" Matthew puzzled.

"Matthew," Jack panicked, "whatever happens, you have to believe me when I say I love you *very* much."

"Dad," Matthew stuttered. "Dad, *you're* scaring me."

"Jack!" Darkmoor called his name again, "aren't you going to face me?"

Matthew narrowed his eyes and stared at his dad. Taking in a few deep breaths, Jack slowly turned to face Darkmoor.

"Hello James!" Jack called over nervously.

Darkmoor smiled, and slowly he bowed his head, "Hello my brother!"